Terror of Breakspear Hall

F.R. Jameson

ISBN: 9798569474158

To V and E, with love, always.

Also by F.R. Jameson in paperback

Ghostly Shadows
Death at the Seaside
Certain Danger
Call of the Mandrake
The Hellbound Detective
The Caller

Screen Siren Noir
Diana Christmas
Eden St. Michel
Alice Rackham

All Ghostly Shadows tales can be read as stand-alone,
but they all take place in the same universe.
Sort of

CHAPTER ONE

God, she was incredible!

Captain Jonathan Datchett drank up the ravishing young lady across the table from him along with his substantial glass of red. She was magnificent! Tall, breathtakingly beautiful and statuesque in the way models in magazines are. In short, she was an absolute goddess. Her face was perfection: high cheekbones, full lips (which always wore a knowing and very sexy smile) and a pair of bright blue feline eyes. Her skin was porcelain and her raven hair so magnificently full and straight he wanted to run his hands through it for hours. (Preferably when it lay on his pillow.) She was the most phenomenal woman he had ever seen.

And she was spending the evening in his company. Despite him being at least forty years older than her and past his prime (but still a vigorous man, he had to admit), this enchanting creature was enjoying an intimate dinner with him. Just the two of them. To all the world a courting couple.

Her laughter was a wondrous symphony. "Oh,

Jonathan, please do tell me another."

In most company, he was parsimonious with his stories. Not sure how the adventurous tales of his youth would play with the soft, bleeding heart generation. But with her, well, he was exceedingly relaxed. She encouraged him, was eager to hear his more dangerous and racy tales. As she was such a rapt audience, he went so far as to relate all his adventures in the last days of Rhodesia. Normally he verbalised none of those experiences – not least because more than one of them could see him marched into a court of law these days – but with her he couldn't stop his tongue from galloping free. She seemed to enjoy them and he wanted more than anything else to make her enjoy herself.

With a titter she leant across the table and stroked her smooth fingers down his. A bolt of electricity passed between them, he felt sure.

The flirtation of her words was impossible to miss. "You really a rogue," she purred.

To think, when the current board of his club suggested allowing women in as guests of members, he was one of loudest objectors. It would destroy the whole character of the place, he argued. He wasn't alone, several old guard made the same protestations. But if it wasn't for that decision being taken against their will, he would never have met Simone.

The wondrous Simone. The sexy Simone. His Simone, as he had started to think of her.

When he first saw her across the floor of the common bar, she was an absolute vision in a blue cocktail dress with its tasselled hem. Her long legs on display, more than a hint of cleavage, but maintaining an elegance and classiness which was an integral part of her being. He caught her eye and, rather magnificently, she caught it right back.

The club member she was accompanying was her idiot brother and she was more than happy to ditch him for Jonathan's company. She explained to Jonathan, as he treated her to more than one martini, that this brother had taken her to a 1920s themed party – hence the dress – but there were no real men there. She placed emphasis on the word 'real'. Annoyed she had asked to go somewhere where she could at least converse with a proper heterosexual member of the male species. (Okay, he allowed, maybe she hadn't quite used *those* words.) Fortunately her idiot brother made his one sensible decision of the year and left the party and brought her to the club he'd recently joined. Not long after she was chatting with Jonathan – as real a man as ever breathed – and her evening was improving.

It was fate.

Now here they were, a few weeks later, the two of them out for a candlelit dinner. This was the fifth evening they'd spent together. He hesitated to call them dates, but more and more in his mind that's what they were becoming.

She sat before him in a low-cut black dress (you have to be careful not to topple in there, old boy) and she was smiling and simpering and making him feel a young buck again.

Judgemental people would say he was a silly old sod to lose his heart to this beautiful young woman. But screw them! They were envious swine.

There was no definite arrangement between them. They weren't calling themselves boyfriend and girlfriend. But the way her eyes sparkled at him across the table, she clearly saw him as something other than a father figure. More than a friend.

However, there was one insect in the ointment: the aforementioned idiot brother. He was a few years younger than Simone, with the same smooth pale skin and full dark hair. Jonathan supposed some might consider him good looking, but to him her brother seemed more a well-groomed nancy-boy.

The brother's name was Robin and he was a blasted do-gooder. He ran his own charitable foundation which did something or other. When he spoke about it, it was with the zeal of a chinless missionary, which meant Jonathan turned himself off after the first sentence. Whenever they met, Robin tried to get Jonathan to make a small contribution. "To keep the lights on," as the young nancy put it. Jonathan had experience with these types before. It was never a *small* contribution they were after, a figure more substantial was always what they meant.

My word! Here was the young nancy now! This was supposed to be a private dinner with Simone, just the two of them. All evening long, gazing lustfully across the table, pretending there was no one else in the world.

Only this *other* had come along. A man who, out of deference to this wonderful creature who had captured his heart, Jonathan couldn't order away in the most fulsome language.

Her brother must have wheedled where they'd be from her. Everyone has a weakness and hers was this ball-less, saintly Samaritan who shared her family name.

"I was passing," Robin told them. "I won't stay long." He said this as he pulled a chair from the next table and plonked it at theirs. Setting it between them. "I have a prior engagement elsewhere, but I was wondering, Johnny, whether you had given any more thought to the Fallowford Trust and all the wonderful work we do."

It took every ounce of self-control not to lash out. To the core of his being, he hated being called Johnny. But with Simone looking absolutely delectable – ravishing across the table from him – he dared not let the merest little squeak of irritation escape.

"I've considered it," Jonathan said, his voice neutral.

"And?" asked Robin. "Come on, don't make me do the hard sell. None of us wants that tonight. I can be gone out of your hair right this instant if you have your cheque book with you, or if you want to make me a promise. I'd accept your word on it, Johnny."

"Go on, Jonathan." Simone licked her carmine lipstick lips and smiled. "It's in a good cause and he does do a lot of really marvellous work." She dropped her voice to a whisper. "Besides, I'm as eager to get rid of him as you are."

She winked at her brother, who beamed at her.

Jonathan gritted his teeth, but smiled. Thinking of having her all to himself. "Alright then," he said. "You wore me down."

He reached into his suit jacket and retrieved his leather-bound chequebook and silver fountain pen. Trying to make it a fluid and relaxed movement, despite it physically hurting him. He always carried his cheque book when paying for a large purchase, such as dinner in a fancy restaurant with a beautiful woman. His was the generation which didn't trust plastics.

With his trusty old pen, which had come with him

to Rhodesia, he wrote a cheque for her brother's damn charity. Five figures. More than good enough to make him disappear into a puff of smoke and think twice before returning with his damn begging bowl.

"Oh, thank you!" The young nancy was delighted. He shook Jonathan's hand, then gave his sister a peck on the cheek. Leaving them – at last! – alone.

Simone reached across the table and squeezed Jonathan's fingers, showing her gratitude. Which gave him a frisson of warmth.

The money might prove to be a sound investment.

Maybe at the end of this night he'd get more than a simple peck on the cheek from this delightful creature.

He could hope.

CHAPTER TWO

Belinda and Robin took a drive into the countryside in her old two-seater MG. Haphazardly following a fold-up map, they chanced upon a delightful looking pub at the edge of a picturesque river. One which had started life as a watermill and retained all the features. They were a little early for food, too early even for the pub to be open. So they parked the car, pulled the roof on and went for a walk in the sunshine. Working up an appetite before they ate. With his arm around her waist and a cheeky glint in his eye, he led through some trees and into a deserted copse. There they made love al fresco. She clutched onto his hips, her nails piercing the material of his shirt as she cried with sheer pleasure. They did it twice, pretending they were sex crazed teenagers.

Lying supine on the grass, breathless, hitching her black lace knickers up before rolling into his arms, she considered herself the luckiest woman in the world. Even though it had been weeks, she still couldn't believe her wonderful fortune.

When they'd met, he'd been quick in signalling his interest in her, but she hadn't quite believed it. He was slim, handsome and much younger than her. Why would he be attracted to a woman who had lost the bloom of youth? The maths embarrassed her whenever she thought of it, but the truth was she was old enough to be his mother.

However, he pursued her, chased her, whispered sweet nothings, until – despite herself – her heart beat faster whenever she thought of him. She tried to play it cool, but from disbelief she moved towards being very, very interested.

In a conversation early in their acquaintance, he'd mentioned his mother died when he was young. She guessed this explained it. What was happening here was an oedipal thing. She felt bad for taking advantage of whatever psychological issues he had buried beneath his suave exterior. More than once she felt it wrong of her. But then, if it wasn't her, it would be another woman the wrong side of the menopause and so she might as well be the one who had the fun.

Besides, she'd fallen quite, quite in love with him.

Obviously she'd had certain inquiries made. She wasn't a complete idiot. But everything he said to her checked out: from the dead parents, to his peripatetic existence and the close relationship to his sister, with whom he ran a charitable foundation.

There was actually a little bit more to his story than he'd told her. An unfortunate incident when he was nineteen years old which didn't seem to be really his fault – carelessness, more than anything – but had got his name into the newspapers. She didn't mind about that as she'd been unlucky enough to have her good name dragged through the press too. Besides the incident explained the certain distant sadness she sometimes felt from him. Without giving it much thought, she decided not to pry. After all his past was his business. The present could be theirs and she was delighted to be enjoying it with him.

Whichever angle she regarded him from, it was impossible to ignore he was gorgeous. A tall slim model of a man with broad shoulders and narrow waist. An Adonis who should sport expensive suits in magazine ads. He had wavy brown hair (which she thought at first looked so good through casual tousling, but the fact it *always* looked that way suggested he in fact used a product she hadn't yet determined.) His eyes were dark chocolate, while his skin was baby smooth. It was almost criminal for any man to have an epidermis as unblemished as he possessed. He was both pretty and handsome; metrosexual, but a manly man. Maybe it was her imagination, her romantic soul running wild, but she thought he had an element of danger to him. He was too young as yet, but if he were ten years older and an actor, he would be a shoo-in for the next James Bond.

(These good genes were a quality which ran in the family, she surmised. She'd been introduced to his older sister, who was almost other-worldly beautiful.)

When Belinda Daindridge was in her twenties, she could never have gone out with a man who looked anything like him. If an Adonis like Robin had made it clear he was interested – which men that handsome never did to shy, wallflower Belinda – then she'd have felt herself too unworthy. She'd have lacked the confidence even to speak to him! (Let alone consider anything more carnal.) But now she felt she was being offered a chance to have the youthful fun she'd denied herself when she actually was a slip of a girl.

It was ironic as the man who had broken her own resistance when she was in her twenties was her husband, Carter, who had been two decades her senior. So it delighted her that the age gap had been reversed and then some.

Not only was Robin easy on the eyeballs, he was a wonderful man. Charming, knowledgeable, an enthralling conversationalist and a wit. No one had ever made her laugh as much as he did. Certainly not old Carter. (She had expected her husband's death would cheer her no end, but his longed for demise turned out to contain a massive sting. She never wanted to talk about it, but the ramifications of it all continued to bother her. Especially the fact people often thought she was more responsible than she actually was because she'd ended up with a lot of money. Yes, Carter had been a crook, but she couldn't be blamed for having the wherewithal to take care of herself.) Robin never enquired into the tricky issue of her past, any more than she asked him about his. Another thing which made her mad about him.

He was admirable too. Running a charity which helped disadvantaged teenagers in the small Kent town in which he was born. Selflessness of that sort was commendable, particularly in one so young. It always impressed Belinda how little he mentioned it. She knew he was always on the hunt for extra funding, this was the nature of the third sector after all. But he never asked her for anything, although she was more than comfortable. However, she'd decided that since they were a couple, the least she could do was help him. Support him. She'd already gifted him one donation from the goodness of her heart (and because her accountant had explained she could write it off), while in her handbag that morning was another cheque with lots of zeroes.

As they lay together post-coital in the fresh air, she imagined the smile which would fill his wonderful face when she handed him the cheque over lunch. Of how thrilled he would be. Maybe, rather than returning to London, they could check into a hotel this afternoon and he could thank her vigorously.

CHAPTER THREE

"Who's next, darling?" asked Simone.

Robin grinned at her across their surprisingly small, twin hotel room. He was knowing and confident, having already worked it out. Probably he'd have liked more space to pontificate, but happily – as well as they were doing – they weren't going to pay the premium rates in this hotel. Each of them had a double bed, there was a wardrobe which would suit their needs and the bathroom wasn't as cramped as she'd have imagined. What more did they really need?

As little children they'd shared a bedroom. That had stopped though as she went through puberty (she was eighteen months and six days older than him), but it had started again when she nursed him after his accident and it had never stopped. Unless they were with someone they were intimate with, then they never went to sleep in different rooms to the other. They took comfort from it. She knew it must appear odd to outsiders for two adult siblings to be sharing a room, but she had gone beyond the point where she cared.

Actually, when they checked in, she'd had other ideas in her mind. The receptionist had been gorgeous. Blonde, chic – with her hair in a beehive transported straight from the 1960s – and a purring French accent to die for. A sparkle in her eyes, Simone had leant on the reception desk and given this Parisian Venus her most flirtatious smile. The lady had smiled back professionally, but also a tad uncomfortable. They chatted for a minute, but Simone didn't push for anything further. Maybe if the two of them got together and shared a bottle of wine then something may have happened, but Simone had grown past the point where she provided straight girls with a racy anecdote they could share later.

Besides which, although it was early days yet, Simone may have met someone.

Still, Robin had teased her about it all the way up in the lift. Saying he'd have to make himself scarce tonight. He was lucky as his type was the matronly woman; he got his thrills from work. Clearly it's what drew him to it. He had a reason to pursue the type of older lady he appreciated, while also getting the comedy value of seeing his gay sister have to make eyes at repulsive walruses who'd prompt her to vomit in any other circumstance.

The way a familiar mischievousness played in his eyes told her the next target was one of the latter.

Simone sat back on her bed, propped herself on her elbows and crossed her legs. She let her shoe dangle off the end of her right foot.

"Who is he?"

He crossed his arms and leant against the wall. Standing next to his bed and the small, square window. "Well, I'm glad you asked, darling."

This afternoon he was intent on being infuriating, as he still didn't provide any answer.

"Am I supposed to guess, Rob?" she asked with barely concealed exasperation.

"I don't think you're that good at guessing, Si. Have you ever heard of a Montagu Breakspear?"

"No," she said. "I'm nowhere good enough at guessing to land upon a name I've never heard before. Who is he and does he have a daughter I can at least make eyes at?"

There was always a smugness to Robin when he told her information she didn't know. The younger brother putting something over on his older sister.

"He has been in the newspapers from time to time," he said, with all the clarity of a man giving hints in a Christmas treasure hunt.

"News, sport or gossip?" she asked.

"Oh, news most definitely. Although the pages would be yellowed."

Of course, Robin had appeared in the newspapers himself in a less than favourable light, but banter though they did, it would have been impolite for her to mention it.

"Thank Christ!" she purred. "The only one you ever got me who was in the sport section was the bloody football manager. I can't go through the hell of trying to bond with another one of those again."

"Don't worry, I wouldn't do that to you. Well, not unless he was spectacularly wealthy and had committed an extremely bad act."

He pulled himself away from the wall and ambled across their room. It wasn't a gigantic space. Between their beds was a small table with an old, plastic, hotel telephone. While on the wall facing their pillows was a mounted TV (they could watch cartoons together if they wanted, she guessed) and, below it, a small cabinet. He sank to his knees and pulled open the cabinet. The eagerness with which he did it made her chuckle. Apparently he expected to find a well-stocked mini-bar. Instead what he found was a small fridge. And even then, one which held nothing more than water, lemonade and orange juice. She nearly laughed out loud at the hurt expression on his face, before remembering it was probably a prelude to him ordering a ridiculously priced beverage through room service. So much for saving money by not springing for the fancy room.

"Who's this Shakespeare then?" she asked, to distract him.

"Breakspear!" he corrected. "And he is the man who inherited and resides in Breakspear Hall."

"Please, darling," she sighed. "Stop speaking in these ridiculous riddles. What the hell is Breakspear Hall?"

But he seemed surprised. "You've never heard of Breakspear Hall?"

"Come on!" She gave a melodramatic eye-roll. "Let me bow to you as the fountain of all wisdom. No need to go through the façade, or to play the game. For the purposes of your various projects, just pretend I am the empty vessel and you can pour your hard-earned knowledge into me."

Robin grinned at her and dropped onto his bed. Lying there with his hands crossed over his chest. It made his voice sound deeper, which is no doubt why he did it.

"I am the resourceful one."

"No, I'm the resourceful one," she reminded him.

"You enjoy the research. Go on then! You have sixty seconds on this Breakspear Hall. No hesitation, repetition or deviation."

"The Breakspear Hall Murders were a notorious trio of killings in 1975."

"Before my time, darling."

"I know, darling, but you have mastered the ability to read, have you not?"

"I have, but I prefer lighter fare. If I want a murder, I'll get it in the pages of Agatha Christie, thank you very much."

"Good thing you have me then." He beamed. "Without my research and my diligence and my willingness to tarnish my mind with all kinds of salaciousness, how would you pay to put those expensive frocks on your back?"

She sat up and let the shoe drop to the floor. "I appreciate your efforts, darling." The smile pained on her face. "Tell me then, what were The Breakspear Hall Murders?"

"Breakspear Hall is an enormous house in South East London. Forest Hill to be exact, but a little way secluded from the suburban part. Until the 1920s it was a boy's school. But something happened there. For the life of me I can't find what. However, the school closed without notice and all the boys were sent away. I had a quick look into it, but then remembered it wasn't pertinent to the money-making schemes of today. Anyway, it's a house which had an oddness attached to it even before the murders."

"Spooky," she said.

"Yeah, sure. Anyway, the headmaster and proprietor were one and the same, he was a Stanley Breakspear, who on his death left it to his son, Walter.

A few years later Walter killed himself and then it went to his nephew, Sebastian."

"You really did go to town on your research, didn't you?" she said, genuinely impressed. "But tell me, darling, why is any of this interesting?"

"Because they were all reclusive men. They all of them shut themselves up from the world and earned a reputation as hermits. And my research was nowhere near as fulsome as you might think. After the murders happened, *The London Chronicle* had a two page article on the history of 'The Death House'. Most illuminating it was. I cribbed everything there."

"That's how you always did your homework, wasn't it?" she laughed. "Skim-read the one thing and hoped it carried you through."

He chuckled with her. "I am better these days. I try to look at three or four sources and read them properly. Besides, this is way more fun than school.

"Anyway," he continued. "In 1975, this Sebastian Breakspear – who although he hid himself from the world, was living in a large manor house in South London and had a good family name – went nuts and in three days killed three random strangers who showed up at his door. One was a salesman, one was a Jehovah's Witness and one was a neighbour who was starting a petition against plans to erect a telephone mast nearby. Each of them came to the door, rang the bell and then Sebastian pulled it back, dragged them in and set upon them with an axe.

"It was the neighbour's wife who called the police. He hadn't come home for dinner and he'd told her before he went out that he would try old Breakspear's place, so they knew where to look. They didn't have to investigate too hard. Within ten minutes of being there they'd found two decapitated bodies stashed in the hedges. The third body – the neighbour's – was also headless, but he was also without arms and legs. There's undoubtedly a different and more comprehensive word for that than just decapitation."

She crinkled her nose in distaste. "What happened then to this Sebastian Breakspear?"

"Died in a hospital before the trial. The defence was all set to enter a plea of diminished responsibility as his mind had snapped, but he also had a degenerative physical condition. Anyway, on his passing, the house – this grand old house in London with the estate and money which accompanied it – was left to his younger brother."

"And this is the Montagu you mentioned?"

"Yes!"

"Right." She drew out the word. "From all you've told me, Rob, I'm not sure he fits into the code. We said we wouldn't punish people for the sins of the father and this is most definitely that."

"Well, here's the interesting thing, darling. This is how Montagu Breakspear ended up in the papers as more than just a footnote to his brother's crimes."

"Go on."

"The families of the victims tried to claim compensation. After all it seemed unlikely this man, who had staff on his payroll, could have reached such a pitch of murderous rage with no one noticing. Given the bodies were ridiculously easy for the police to find, you'd have thought the butler would have noticed them while gazing through the window and polishing the silver.

"After Sebastian's death, the families tried to get recompense for the grievous injury they'd suffered.

Montagu blocked them at every turn. He claimed there was no money, that there was only the house which was in a terrible state of disrepair and wouldn't be worth much on the open market. Besides which, it was his old family home and, despite Sebastian's crimes, it should stay in the family. In short, it shouldn't under any, any circumstance be taken off him. He should stay there and bring it back to its splendour and eventually separate off part of the grounds as a memorial garden to the victims. That would be his heartfelt tribute."

"Let me guess," she said. "The twist of the story is he didn't do any of what he promised?"

"Correct, darling. Nor, as far as I can tell, did he make the token donation to the various charities which he claimed he would. Well, not unless he kept it quiet. And since for a short period of time all kinds of people were baying at him to do 'the right thing', discretion and modesty would seem a poorly timed tactic."

Simone glanced through the small window at the slate grey sky of London. "Maybe he was telling the truth? Maybe the house was a wreck and there wasn't much in the way of inheritance? Come on, we know as well as anyone else how forefathers can squander an inheritance."

"If it was a wreck in 1975, how could he be still living there today? It should be a ruin. If his finances are in a dire state, why is he in a private casino at least one evening a week? Why is he accompanied by his own personal butler?"

Her eyebrow rose in a perfect arch. "Not the same one, surely?"

"I wouldn't have thought so," he said. "But a butler is a butler. New or old, they're the last word in pampered luxury."

Every so often she objected to his plans. Occasionally she even derailed them. His excitement was far too high on this one though. She might have had an odd feeling about it, but since there was no genuine reason for her to have an odd feeling, she knew she'd be going along with his scheme. This Montagu Breakspear fellow was their next target.

"Okay," she said, fixing him with her full attention. "Let's get ready for work. What does he like?"

Robin beamed at her. "He's not a man who gives interviews or has flattering profiles written about him. We will have to wing this one by our earlobes."

"Give me a hint then, darling. Anything would help. Is his preference boys or girls?"

It's hard work to shrug your shoulders while lying prone on a bed, but Robin managed it. "Really, I have no idea. He might like both, or neither. He keeps himself to himself. I think we're both going to have to look delicious and see which one he stares at longest."

This had been their modus operandi before, but it was impossible not to shudder a little at his stating it out loud. "Fine." Then she repeated the mantra which had become a private joke between them, her voice flat: "We can take on anyone. We can take on the world."

He beamed at her, missing the sarcasm

"Where are we going to find this private person?" she asked.

"He may not be a social animal, but he's a member and regular patron of Henman's Casino."

Her eyebrow raised. "Why do I know that name?"

"It's where we met Thomas McGinty."

"Ah," she said. "Will that be a problem? Might we not run into him?"

"Heart attack," Robin said. "Near fatal. He's recuperating in the West Country. Do you want me to send a bouquet, darling?"

She remembered a short, squat, bald man with lots of hands. "Make it anonymous," she said.

"Will do." He smiled.

"So, when shall we try for this Breakspear?" she asked.

"No time like the present, darling. Tonight?"

She resisted a frown. They never took much of a break. "Fine. I better get myself ready."

"Yes. As I say, tonight we both have to radiate sex appeal and charm. If one of us isn't turning the old bastard's head, we're doing something wrong."

Simone went to the bathroom first, but didn't let on that her shoulders slumped the moment the door closed.

CHAPTER FOUR

Jasper Redditch always hated the way his cousin Belinda smirked at him. She'd done it for as long as he could remember, always thinking she was better than him. It was smug, arrogant, condescending and judgmental. Making it clear she was peering down her nostrils at the poor relation. That she was only tolerating his intrusion into her time, and the way she'd get through it was to laugh about it with her friends later. Like the bitch she was.

"This is serious, Belinda." He was trying to be reasonable. Only letting a little wisp of irritation seep out.

"Oh, it is?" She could barely stop herself laughing in response.

She was always so bloody superior to him. Her father was their Grandpa's favourite child. There were three children of the old man. Marcus, who was Belinda's dad; William, who instilled the values of hard work and decency in his son, Jasper; and at the end, Cece. Years younger than her brothers, and there to be adored by Grandpa – while not taken seriously.

In Grandpa's firm, it was William who actually did all the work, but it was Marcus who was unfairly given all the respect. Even though he was a playboy with no more brains in his head than it took to tie a tennis shoe. It was William who kept the company afloat when Grandpa's business acumen failed him. William who gave his entire being to the family firm.

There was no thank you for dedication though.

Indeed, such was the iniquity of the legacy, it was Uncle Marcus who was left the majority of Grandpa's estate. There was a pittance to Jasper's dad, and even less to Cece. Although Grandpa did at least ensure she had married well.

It meant there was enmity in the family. A grudge filled dislike which was passed down a generation. Really, as near contemporaries, Belinda and Jasper should have been allies. In another version of reality they might have been friends. But Belinda, through slight age difference and the lineage bestowed upon her by her adored father, decided her superiority to him. She had taken that stance when she was a child and, fifty years later, she wasn't letting it go.

Jasper was the upstart, scruffy, poor relation. She could have cruel fun with him as much as she liked.

If he'd had his way, he'd have done anything not to speak to her. He was a man who welcomed a peaceful life, after all. But it had come to his attention that she seemed to be frittering away what was left of the family fortune right through her chubby fingers.

She grinned at him. "This is none of your business, Jasper."

This was another thing which irritated him. The way she stretched the sound between the s and the p in his name. Giving the impression it was sullying her mouth by being there.

"I think it very much is my business," he told her.

"How? It's my money."

"It was our grandfather's money. Just because your father was older, it doesn't mean I don't have a claim. Who worked harder for the company? My dad or yours?"

She rolled her eyes. One more thing to infuriate him.

"You cling to this strange notion, Jasper, but you're well aware grandfather's famed fortune was nothing to write home about at his passing. And what was left, dear Daddy let slip through his fingers. The money I have comes from my husband."

"And where did your lovely hubby get it from?" he snapped. "Anyone ever looked into that, Belinda?"

It was a low blow, but one she'd pushed him into taking.

She pouted at him unimpressed, while secretly his heart leapt.

This wet Thursday afternoon he had driven right across London to see her. From the small suburban house he had been proud to buy himself in Woolwich, to the riverside flat she certainly didn't deserve in Richmond. When he'd rung the buzzer and told her who it was, she'd hesitated. Made him wait a good thirty seconds, considering whether to give a dismissive "Not today, thanks!" and send him bloody packing.

Well, she'd finally recognised sense (and friendly manners) and let him in. What he found inside was a mess. Didn't people who had money pay for cleaners anymore? Wasn't she capable of putting things away herself? Couldn't she wash a dish? The clutter of the place was no doubt accentuated by the way her lounge bled into her kitchen which then spilled into dining area. Open plan was what they called it, but he liked proper boundaries. He had to say that some of the art on the walls suggested a good eye. Particularly an English pastoral scene of a river which – showing off, no doubt – still had the price-tag attached. He'd be happy to have one or two pieces hung on the walls of his own abode. But to keep a home in this terrible clutter was obscene.

And that's before he got a good look at what her latest makeover had done to her.

What did the old trout look like? In her tight black skirt and thin red blouse, a material flimsy enough he could see her black lace bra underneath (and it must have been straining to hold her saggy udders). She resembled a mobile hairdresser. An especially cheap and slutty hairdresser. One who was having a mid-life crisis and thus was trying too hard. How old did she think she was?

For himself, Jasper had embraced the passing years. He'd actually welcomed the baldness and the rounding of his belly. Not her, she looked as if she was intent on disporting herself on a discotheque dancefloor and embarrassing anyone unfortunate enough to witness the display.

The notion flashed across his mind that she'd found herself a man and he was what all this was in aid of. But no, such a concept was ridiculous. Who would look at her twice? You can dress an old cow as a prostitute, but an old cow is all she would be.

She stood up from her soft Swedish furnishings armchair and ran her hands down the front of her skirt.

Probably not wanting to let the material bunch too far around her thunder thighs.

"It's always an experience to see you, Jasper." Her voice was a spoonful of poison. "But next time call ahead, or maybe don't come at all. I'm a busy woman and I don't have all the time in the world to deal with your nonsense."

But he wasn't one to be brushed off easily.

He slammed his hand on her kitchen table. "Where's the fucking money, Belinda? What have you done with it?"

Her body tensed and he saw she was counting down from five beneath her breath. "It's my money and I will do with it as I wish."

"Oh, I'm sorry, do you have any kids suddenly I don't know of? I'm next of kin, Belinda, in case you've forgotten. When you're out and about cavalierly spending every pound you can get your hands on, then it affects me too."

"Ha! Jasper, I assure you, you are not getting a penny."

It was her coolness which did it. She kept her head level and her jaw tight, while her eyes were full of righteousness. Her voice did not rise, but this was a line drawn to end the argument. If she'd yelled at him, then he would have yelled back. Insults could have been hurled between them until the neighbours banged on the walls to stop the noise. Undoubtedly things would then have been better. They'd have let off steam and regrouped with a certain grudging friendliness. Everything in the open, so they could move on. That's how it played out during previous disagreements. But the fact she was contemptuously trying to get rid of him, that she was going to show him to the door as an unwelcome guest, that she would try and scrape him off her shoes, well, it made him explode inside.

Before he knew what he was doing, he took two steps forward and punched her full in the face.

It was with no forethought. Beforehand, he would never have considered himself a violent man. But she had pushed him too far and he had to act. If he hadn't responded, how would he have confronted his own gaze in the mirror?

The blow struck her full in the left eye. He snagged his hand back, then realised his gold signet ring had caught her eyelid. Half her fake eyelashes peeled off, taking the skin behind with them, and sprayed blood down that slutty top of hers.

Still, she took the blow with a gasp rather than a scream. A sharp intake of breath and then she stood and stared at him, confusion in her unspoiled right eye. Crimson ran down her face and the remains of her left eyelid fluttered in the breeze, but Belinda stood before him silent. It was disconcerting. The sheer rage which was pumping within meant he had dealt his best shot. He couldn't hit any harder. He'd hurt her, but instead of collapsing as she should have done, she remained facing him. Continuing to sneer at her poor cousin. With her one undamaged pupil, she was handing him another withering glare. A dismissive – oh so superior – smirk crossing her lips.

The thought of it made him come to boil once more. Taking one step back and then lurching himself forward, he punched her full in the mouth and felt her two front teeth detach themselves with a crack. He clasped his knuckles; bruises already rising on them.

Then she went down. Toppling backwards over the armchair and landing with an ungainly thud on the faux wooden flooring she seemed to love.

She screamed finally.

Part of him was jubilant. It meant he had got to her. At last she was paying serious attention to him. But this flat wasn't big and, despite its price tag, its walls weren't too thick. Any neighbour loitering at home was bound to be wondering what the hell was going on with the fat cow.

Jasper moved. A boot into her side, a lesson it would be in her best interests to shut her noise. The lesson didn't immediately take, so he kicked her again. This time, going for the source of the cacophony and his toe-cap catching her full in the face. He put everything he could into it and felt her head judder to the right.

There was silence for a minute. The only noise was Jasper's own breathing as he peered down at her. This wasn't the way he had wanted his afternoon to go. When he arrived, he thought they'd be able to talk things through, that Belinda would see sense and stop being extravagant. But she was far too unreasonable a human being and matters had spun out of control. It wasn't his fault though. He was a victim of circumstance.

Was she dead?

He couldn't tell and somehow considered it would be distasteful to get on his hands and knees and try to listen for any breath coming from between her swollen lips. He thought she was dead and didn't feel sad about her demise, but considered he should make bloody sure. Throughout his working life, Jasper Redditch had prided himself on never leaving a job half done and this was no exception.

He raised his right foot and smashed it on to her

upturned face. Rendering her nose a splattered pulp and sending the cartilage like a hammer into her brain. Thank god he had worn his black trousers and black boots that morning. Hopefully the blood stains wouldn't show.

It turned out to be cathartic.

Once he started stomping her, he couldn't stop. With every kick, her face got softer beneath his heel. The bones bruised then bent then broke then smashed into what seemed like a hundred unique pieces. He watched as her skin erupted in an angry purple, before deflating before his eyes. All ballast behind collapsing in on itself, leaving a misshapen bag attached to an improperly dressed middle-aged woman's body.

Not once did he feel any regret. There was no remorse. He realised later there had been an excitement, but it was the adrenalin flowing more than anything else. No, the dominant emotion he experienced was relief. He would never have to deal with Belinda and her nastiness again. She'd pushed him into it, but it was the right thing to do. The thought occurred if he'd killed her a long time ago, he'd have led a happier life.

Once he'd finished, when he felt he didn't have the strength to do anymore, he made himself a cup of tea and sat on the Swedish couch. It took him a few moments to find the remote, but then he switched the TV on. In one cupboard he came across four of those French macarons, which she must have bought fresh that morning from one of the fancy shops in Richmond. He ate all of them and watched a home improvement show. Completely forgetting about Belinda's body mere inches from his feet as he got lost in this silly, gay, Scottish couple, blowing their budget as they tried to renovate a farmhouse in the Highlands.

He knew he had to move, to discover what Belinda had been doing with the family money. It was a pleasant surprise to him then that in the ugly clutter of her flat, he located her bank statements easily.

They did not make pleasant reading. A good chunk of money had gone to Sariah, his little, ever hungry cousin. Of course it had. Sariah had always been a greedy bitch and Belinda, being a bitch herself, pampered her.

But he also saw two surprisingly large payments had been made to something calling itself The Fallowford Trust. Four hundred thousand in total.

What the fuck was The Fallowford Trust?

Jasper Redditch determined to find out.

CHAPTER FIVE

Simone was impressed by her first sight of Montagu Breakspear. Seen across the dark floor of the basement casino, he had a certain presence to him. A vigour which wasn't often found in men over eighty years old.

Undeniably his skin was wrinkled and liver spots were visible across his hands and face. The skin around his eyes had thinned, which meant they had a certain hollowed out redness. What must once have been attractive thick lips had thinned with the years, lending his whole expression a forever austere look.

Yet there was a certain forcefulness to him. Despite his age, he had lost no height. He was a well-proportioned six foot four. (If he had lost height, he would have been an absolute giant of a man when young.) There was no stoop to his shoulders or spine, so even today he walked with a military bearing. There was a cane in his hand, but it was a prop as much as anything else. His hair was snow white and had receded from his forehead, but the rest could be described as thick and lustrous. She thought, if styled right, he could sport one of those halfway over the head old man quiffs.

The end effect was he was a man who caught the eye. Men never did anything for her, but she could say whether or not one was handsome. She wouldn't have called Montagu Breakspear handsome, but in his salad days – in a saturnine fashion – she could see how he'd make a straight woman's knees go weak.

The point Robin had made about his money was also clear. He was not a man who appeared poor. That evening he was dressed in a white tuxedo, with a red cummerbund. It was not a suit purchased off the rack, but one which had been tailored for him. Added to the ensemble was the cane with its gleaming gold handle and the manicured nails she spotted when she first ventured near him. All of which suggested Montagu Breakspear – despite claims to the contrary – was doing very well for himself, thank you very much.

Compared to others at the casino, he stood out. Even if dress rules had been relaxed since she was last there. Across those two ridiculously easy nights they had ensnared Thomas McGinty, ties weren't required, but suits were. However, even this nod to formality seemed to have been abandoned. With more than one hungry looking gambler trying to find his lucky table in sports jacket and chinos.

This old, dapper gent moving through the throng was incongruous. A character from a 1930s screwball comedy transported into the present. Not the lead, but a side character who sneered at the lead for most of the film, but would turn out to have a heart of gold. Well, hopefully this Montagu Breakspear did have a generous spirit. The orphaned children of Fallowford needed another cheque.

It was the case Simone was striking that evening as well. The red dress she'd fished out of her travelling wardrobe looked shiny and brand new. She had worn it on lots of occasions, but was skilled at maintaining her clothes. It was too tight and tantalisingly low-cut – just on the point of being indecent, but not quite. In a place such as this, it gained her a lot of attention. But she had long practiced keeping her face indifferent and not acknowledging any of the eager smiles or nods. If one of those bastards approached her with a cheesy line, she didn't respond. Just froze them with a glare which was abyssal. There was only one man she wanted to pay her attention tonight. Only she had to be subtle about it. Or as subtle as any woman in an electric red tight dress could be.

However, her first attempt to make an impression didn't seem to land. Simone stood next to Breakspear at the craps table. Right beside his left arm, beaming with excitement as he rolled. She didn't touch him, but she was close enough for the molecules between them to vibrate. Luck wasn't on his side and she sighed sympathetically. And more than loud enough for him to hear.

He turned and regarded her. His face held rigid, but she thought he wouldn't be able to help but give an appraising gaze. Good or bad, he'd want to make something of this young lady getting so close she was practically giving him a massage. The two of them locked eyes for an instant and she beamed at him. Hoping for an appreciative smile in response. A hint of a younger wolf deep inside, flattered by the attention. Instead his visage stayed stony. Hostile even. He watched her from under those red eyelids as if planning to have her burned at the stake. Then he put the dice onto the edge of the table, pressed his cane into the soft carpet and walked away. Leaving her grinning into air, a flirtatious idiot. She hoped none of the other losers around her took it as encouragement.

It wasn't necessarily a problem. They'd encountered this kind of thing before. An older man – one aware he was past his prime, or maybe who had never had a good opinion of his looks anyway – who could not believe a young, attractive female would offer him any time. That she'd have even a passing interest in him. Such men were immediately (and let's be fair, in this case, justifiably) suspicious of it.

It was also a fact some men appreciated the company of other men more. Not in a gay way necessarily, but in the sense of a younger man they could bond with. A vigorous and handsome buck who they could pretend reminded them of their youthful selves.

It would be up to Robin to work his magic now. The casino itself was underground, but the bar was another floor below. Properly subterranean, so much so they called it The Dungeon. A dark little palace of men, which once upon a time would have billowed with cigar smoke.

Robin was already there, leaning against the bar itself. Stood with his traditional whisky sour. He didn't glance at her when she rested next to him and ordered her own glass of champagne. No, he was a man minding his own business. Gazing around the casino bar despondently, a chap who had lost a sum of money perhaps. So self-absorbed, you'd think he wouldn't even notice Montagu Breakspear amble in.

There was a good half an hour when Montagu Breakspear walked between tables and checked out the various games. For a man who had been a member of the casino (Robin had somehow determined) for more than half a century, he didn't seem to know anyone there. There were no friendly smiles or nods in anyone's direction. He was a stranger amongst strangers. Nor did he gamble much. There was a throw of the craps here, one hand of blackjack there and an almost bored spin of the roulette wheel. He didn't commit to anything. He didn't give the impression of a man who enjoying gambling.

In common with most casinos, the only seats available on the game floor itself were for those men and women who properly wanted to risk their money. Not for the dabblers. So they knew this old man on a cane would not stay up there forever. He'd come down, rest his weary legs and pay for an extortionately priced drink.

Simone had already had her shot and not succeeded, but Robin was ready.

Not looking in the right direction, he nevertheless watched Breakspear come into the bar and disdainfully examine the small clutter of round tables. There was only one free, with two chairs, which worked for them perfectly. Breakspear gained a bit of speed as he moved over to it. In case there was someone caddish enough to steal it from an octogenarian. Which with the venue the way it was these days, wasn't out of the question. He got his prize though, took his seat and then summoned across the tiny, dirty blonde waitress to take his order. For her he managed what seemed his first smile of the evening. Though the thinness of his lips and his teeth worn down towards the jaw, meant it wasn't the most pleasant of sights. He ordered a bottle of French champagne and the waitress dashed to oblige.

Robin waited for the bottle to arrive and the contents to be sipped and tasted, before he made his move.

It was the perfect time of the evening. The first wave of gamblers through the door had hit a lull. There were a few upstairs still riding a lucky streak, but the rest were downstairs regrouping themselves. It made Robin's request all the more simple.

"Excuse me, old sport," he beamed. "You wouldn't mind if I took the other spot at this table, would you?"

Eyes narrowed, Breakspear regarded Robin's open, smiling face, then immediately glared to Simone, who was standing as unobtrusively as a woman in a bright red dress can stand.

The two of them had been cautious not to glance at each other, but somehow he had seen the connection.

Breakspear pointed at her, his voice a loud bass which rumbled right across the room: "You're with *that* young lady, aren't you?"

To his credit Robin didn't let his smile falter, kept his face non-committal.

The old man sniffed. "Well, your lack of an answer is an answer all in itself. You may as well invite her to the table. I don't know what it is, but the two of you clearly want something with me, so we may as well get it done with, hadn't we?"

CHAPTER SIX

"I presume you are representatives of the press?"

His voice was rich, a musical instrument. A resounding deep timbre which should have belonged to a much younger man.

Robin had smiled and apologised and borrowed a chair from a couple of Chinese businessmen at the next table. After strolling from the bar, Simone had taken the seat across from Breakspear. He fixed her with angry eyes, disapproval etched into the wrinkles of his face. From her there was no nervousness. She didn't wince, but met his gaze. Seemingly in utter control.

"Do we strike you as press?" she asked.

"Yes!" Robin chuckled at the notion. "The journalists I've encountered have been pale fellows with dandruff and a polite sense of poverty. Men – and I guess women – who type about life rather than living it."

"Anyone can spruce themselves up for a night out," Breakspear replied.

"Tell me," Simone said, leaning forward and resting

her chin on her hand. Giving him a rapt, beautiful gaze. "Have you had much experience with the newspapers?"

She saw him suppress a morbid smirk. He didn't answer her question; thus reminding her of a Cabinet Minister she had once endured three evenings with. Instead, he reposted with, "The fact you can provide an expert description of the journalistic profession suggests you two have also had dealings with the vultures. Am I correct?"

Robin kept smiling. He gave no other reaction.

"We're not reporters, or columnists, or photographers, or bloggers, or podcasters, or humble historians," Simone told him. "We are merely people in a casino."

"People interested in me?"

"All I did, old chap," said Robin, chuckling, "was ask you for a seat."

Breakspear snorted, unimpressed, disbelieving. "What is the relationship between you two? Is it siblings, or is it cousins? There's a striking resemblance, whatever."

"She's my sister."

Breakspear turned his gaze on Simone. "You made sure you got yourself noticed up there at the tables. In my youth, I had the occasional woman who made overt advances towards me. It brought back sweet memories and, at the same time, set off a klaxon.

"Then," he pointed at Robin, "this young scamp comes and tries to join my table. You must believe I have lost my faculties, or at least my eyesight, to think you would get away with a ploy so obvious."

"We're only trying to be friendly," assured Robin.

"Hah!" scoffed the old man. He hadn't yet touched

his champagne, but now reached with a shaky hand and, after slowly ascending the glass to his lips, took a large mouthful.

Earlier she'd been impressed by the steadiness of his hands. They were obviously getting to him in one way, even if it wasn't the way they wanted.

Leaning forward, Simone tried her best smile. "Is it really hard to believe we might simply be friendly?"

"No one wants to be friends with me!" he opined, in his rumbling tones. "At least not without an ulterior motive and I'm yet to determine what yours might be."

"I think you're being a little hard on yourself…" Robin began.

Breakspear held up his palm to stop him. "Do you know how I know it to be true?" he asked. "It is true because I am old. Impossibly old. It is inconceivable young people such as yourselves would look at me and not see the spectre of death. It clings to my bones. It is around me as a constant, unyielding companion. So no, I do not believe anyone will try to become my friend through sheer good-heartedness. As deep down they'd be afraid death was catching."

Simone sat back and took a sip of her own champagne. "You must be a joy to have at parties."

No one else would have noticed, but she could sense Robin wince beside her.

"I don't go to parties, Miss."

"Maybe," she said, "if you were a more open and friendly person, you'd get invites to parties. You would have more friends."

Moving quicker than most men of his vintage, he slammed the base of his cane into the carpet and stood. His tall frame towering over them.

"Miss, I am not in the market for any friends.

Absolutely not. Besides which, I know no one will make friends with me, unless they want something. You have an ulterior motive of sorts. And unless you are prepared to tell me what it is, then I think this finishes this conversation, don't you?"

He took a long stride past them and headed towards the exit, leaving most of his bottle of champagne behind.

"Goodbye, Mr Breakspear!" she called after him.

Once more Robin winced beside her. Although this time it was eminently noticeable.

Breakspear spun around on his cane and glared at them. His heavy brow lined with formidable rage. It was as if a thousand questions jumped in the air for him, but he didn't utter one. Instead he turned and just stalked off into the night.

Waiting until Breakspear was in the lift and on his way to the casino or civilisation, Robin held his hands wide in the universal 'what the hell?' gesture.

Simone chuckled. "Well, he was a charm, wasn't he, darling?"

"You said his name, Si." Robin rarely used a reprimanding tone. Perhaps because he knew it didn't suit him. "Which I think blows all chances straight from the water."

"At least he'll remember us." She gave a shrug of her shoulders. "And as you've said many times, it's better to intrigue than be forgettable." She pushed Breakspear's glass in Robin's direction. "Besides, do you think the 'oh, we're just interested in you for you' approach is going to be effective after this evening's scene?"

"I put a lot of work into him, Si."

"Oh, come on, darling. You did a lot of research.

It's not the same thing." She finished her own glass of champagne in a long, cool sip and then reached across and topped up with the old man's bottle. "Who's plan B? There's always a plan B, isn't there?"

He grimaced, before relaxing his shoulders and taking a big gulp of Breakspear's glass. "It's actually another member of this place. Funnily enough, he's here tonight."

"Really?" she asked, rolling her eyes. "Okay, but as Napoleon may or may not have once said, not tonight. I just want to drink this very fine vintage and not think about work."

He nodded and took another deep gulp. Then, with a certain thoughtfulness added: "You know what, considering it from top to bottom, maybe the old man isn't a blown chance."

"Seriously?" she asked. "You think so?"

"As you said, we must have made him a little curious."

CHAPTER SEVEN

Despite all the money her idiot parents had spent on her education, Jasper Redditch's young cousin Sariah was nothing more than a cheap slattern. She may have the proper cut-glass accent and friends with ridiculous names like Felix and Tarquin – she might even have used her connections to nab herself a nebulous job in The City and the fancy flat in Chelsea to go with it – but Sariah had tawdry written across every inch of her anorexic frame.

She was a good twenty years younger than him. Aunt Cece's late in life accidental little sprog. As such, he'd known her since she was a baby. Even then he'd not thought much of her. She'd been greedy, but not in the way which apparently makes a chubby child a delight to watch. No, she'd been greedy for other people's possessions. There was one time when he couldn't leave her family home after a visit as she'd taken his car keys and hidden them at the bottom of her toy box. Not because she liked him and wanted him to stay, but because she'd fancied the look of them.

The bitch!

His mistake with Belinda was he'd imagined she'd be reasonable. He had expected too much of her. Even if things had gone differently in Richmond yesterday, he would never make the same error with Sariah. She was the kind of person who gave selfishness a terrible name. There'd be no persuading her something she considered hers wasn't actually hers. So he might as well save time and go to her flat when she wasn't there and discover what he could concerning the whereabouts of his money.

The last twenty-four hours for Jasper had not been as difficult as he envisaged. After Richmond, he'd rushed back to his tiny house in Woolwich and tried to concoct an alibi. Give him a story to tell the police when they came. But there was no knock on his door. And when he searched online he could find no report of a murder in Richmond. That meant they hadn't found her yet! He pictured her body lying stiff and broken on her floor. Undiscovered, as of now. For the moment he was clear.

This fact would change. It might not have looked that way, but he was sure Belinda had a cleaner. Someone would open her front door and gasp at her smashed in corpse. Maybe it would only be when the bluebottles started swarming, but it would happen. Yesterday he had considered charging straight to Sariah's place, but then talked himself out of it – imagining how bad it would appear in a court of law if he seemed to be on a kind of crime spree. But after a night of seething on it and a bag packed in the back of his car, so he could run to the airport if need be, he knew he had to do it. This unexpected window of opportunity meant luck was finally going his way. No more half measures then, he had to get what was his.

Taking the crowbar from the boot of his car and checking over both shoulders to make sure he wasn't observed, he snuck around to the back door of her basement flat and prised it open, the door-jamb splintering. Given how much the rent would be on her ridiculously small flat, it was embarrassing how easy it was to break into. She didn't even have an alarm.

What he found inside he should have predicted, yet it shocked him.

Compared even to Belinda, she lived in the squalor of an utter pig.

He came in through the kitchen and there were dirty dishes and plates all across the work surfaces. *All* the work surfaces. In addition, she'd piled the sink high with other pots, pans and utensils. The four rings of the hob were barely visible under a several layers of grease; while he was glad he paid attention to where he placed his feet, as he almost trod on a slice of what appeared to be peanut butter on toast which had been dropped to the floor and left there. What made it worse was it appeared to have been there for days. How could she live in this fashion? To not only drop it there, but to walk past it repeatedly and be too indolent to pick it up.

He placed his crowbar on one of the few clear spots on the kitchen cabinets and, steeling himself, ventured into the rest of her flat.

The bedroom was only a surprise in that there weren't dirty, used sex toys strewn around the floor. She had an enormous wardrobe and a giant Chinese laundry basket, but most of her garments were in crumpled piles. He saw a pair of knickers which were unspeakably stained and nearly made him regurgitate his breakfast.

His own place was spotless. He prided himself on it. It embarrassed him to be related to this creature.

Say what you would on the subject of Belinda – and he had and would continue to do so – but when he had stepped back to look at her residence, he had found her paperwork easily. There was no such simple task in Sariah's hovel. He guessed the lounge would be the best place to start, but unless she was filing them under the dirty sofas, or in the overflowing magazine racks, or – most incredibly – in the old pizza boxes stacked in the corner, then nothing was readily apparent.

He didn't want to tear her whole flat apart though. Partly because he didn't want her to realise it was him who had been there, but mostly – he realised – he didn't want to touch anything.

Still it was money which was rightfully his and he'd gone through a lot for it already. If he had to sweep soiled undies out of the way to look under her bed, then that's what he would do.

Jasper Redditch was not a man afraid to get his hands a little smudged.

He was on all fours on her bedroom floor, when he heard the key turn in her front door and then it slam behind her. He didn't have time to do more than straighten up on his knees before the skinny, stuck-up bitch stood in the doorway goggling at him with shocked, appalled amazement.

"What the fuck do you think you're doing? Perv!"

It had been quite a few years since he'd seen her, but – my word! – Sariah looked a state. It was like that silly country singer said: all the money she had and she spent it on appearing utterly cheap. Her blonde hair was artificially light and artificially long, extensions trailing down her shoulders. Her white top didn't have enough material to cover her midriff (and showed off the tail of an ugly snake tattoo rising above her left hip), while her faded jeans had numerous holes torn into their front. Then there was the face. As far as he was concerned, there was classy and understated make-up, and then there was letting a group of toddlers with crayons loose on yourself. She was definitely the latter.

But right then, as much as it pained him, the stupid little cow had the upper hand. Lord knows what she was doing home (day's holiday, called in sick, been fired perhaps), yet it meant she could stare at him with righteous fury. He had broken in and he was scrabbling around on her bedroom floor. Despite his motives being decent, she would never see things his way.

She took a pace back into the hallway, reached into her handbag and he feared she might grab some mace or a rape alarm. Instead it was her phone. Thumb heading to dial 999.

Jasper held out his hands, appearing friendly. They were more than friends, they were family. He smiled at her. His welcoming smile.

"Sorry to startle you. I'm just checking in on you, cousin," he said. "I was in the neighbourhood and wanted to see how the wealthy half lives."

A snarl welded itself to her face, but her thumb stopped its motion. He noticed she no longer had the dignity to wear a bra when she went onto the street.

"Tell me one fucking reason I don't call the police on you, Jasper. What the fuck is this? How the fuck did you get in?"

She hadn't glanced yet into the kitchen and seen the broken in back door.

The smile stayed on his face, hurting his cheeks.

"I'm sorry," he said. "This is all underhand and I apologise. But I was sent here and I was told to be as discreet as possible. When you weren't home, I'm afraid I let myself in."

"What? Who sent you?"

He swallowed, but knew at the same time none of his story would ever be contradicted. "Who else? Belinda."

"Belinda?" she screeched. When talking normally, Sariah's accent was cut glass enough to sound a parody of itself. However, when she yelled, the inner trollop floated to the surface.

"Yes." Jasper stood gingerly. "I've been speaking to Belinda and she's worried. Things are a little tighter in her finances than she would wish. So, and this is embarrassing for me to say, she was wondering what happened to all the money she gave you. She'd appreciate as much of it back as possible."

"What?" Sariah yelled again.

His hands up, palms out to convey no threat, he took a step towards her. "Terrible investments, I'm afraid. Belinda has acknowledged she hasn't been as clever as she should have been. She finds herself short and, the way she sees it, the money she gave you was a loan. To be honest, she's embarrassed for not making the fact as clear to you as she should have done. That's why she sent me, rather than come herself. It was a loan and now she wants it back. So what say you? Are you able to give me a lump sum today to pass onto her and then we can arrange instalments for the rest?"

Mouth open, Sariah gawped at him from the hallway. The little tart had never been the brightest of girls and he could see the cogs turning. He imagined he could smell smoke as the sparks inside the thing she called a brain flickered into life. It took a minute, before she fixed him with utter contempt.

"Oh, fuck off, Jasper!" she yelled. "This is you, isn't it? Belinda would never have sent *you* as a messenger for anything. And she doesn't care about the money. When she gave it to me, she told me I should have the time of my fucking life with it."

"Really…" he began, about to tell her this had been Belinda putting on a front.

She cut him off, taking a step towards him. Jaw raised with defiant righteousness. "When she gave me the fucking money, her only stipulation was I throw a gigantic party and invite her. That was it. I threw one and I invited her and she had a fucking great time. As did the Spanish waiter she woke up with."

Of course Belinda did that, thought Jasper. Not just mutton dressed as lamb, but mutton which imagined it could prance around the meadows as lamb.

"Besides," Sariah continued, her anger building, "if she had a problem with me, she'd never have sent *you* to deal with it. Never in ten trillion fucking years! She hates you as much as I do."

There was only three feet between them. The façade of a smile had vanished from Jasper's face. They were glaring at each other.

"Face it, Jasper!" Sariah spat. "You're a fucking weirdo! A cheap, depressing, creepy fucking miser, who puts his nose into everyone else's business as he has no life and no fucking personality of his own! You're a worthless piece of shit with no friends and so you have to bother those of us unfortunate enough to be in your family, as you've nothing else to do. You're a pathetic waste of a man and it embarrasses me to be related to you!"

It was then he hit her. As ugly as her words were, her stupid tart's face – with all its gaudy make-up – was worse and he couldn't bear it any longer. He couldn't stand the sanctimonious superiority in her eyes. So to shut her up and make her realise he was in charge, not her, he belted her full in the mouth.

Her head jerked back and it might have seemed comic at another time. Sariah deciding to make a spontaneous examination of the ceiling. She didn't fall though. And when her face came back towards him, her snarl was animalistic. Two lines of blood dribbled from her lips where he'd cut them.

Sariah lurched forward and spat full in his face. Splattering him with reddened phlegm. A disgusting gift from a truly disgusting person.

He flinched, wiping his eyes, crying with disgust and shock.

It was then she grabbed him. Being the girl she was, she liked to pull hair. That's the fighting she went for. She swung her hand wide and slammed it onto the top of his head. But his hair was – apart from a few tufts above his ears – a distant memory. So her nails sank into his bare scalp.

Yelling in pain and frustration, Jasper used his right arm, reaching up to pull her off him, while his left went for her bare waist, determined to wrestle her to the floor.

The bitch – for such an emaciated female – was stronger than he expected.

In the doorway of her bedroom the two of them grappled. Neither of them gaining an immediate advantage: scratching, pushing and kicking. He pulled her hand from his bare scalp and felt his own blood drip from his head. But then she tried to gouge his left eye. Her painted fake talons like those of a beast from folklore. He responded by punching her full in the stomach and feeling gratified when she buckled.

It gave him the advantage and he pushed her, the two of them taking the half dozen steps from the bedroom into the lounge. Picking up speed as he propelled her backwards, until she toppled over a footstool. Landing with a crash of the dirty plates she'd piled there.

She screamed as she fell. But grabbed onto him and yanked him all the way with her.

Jasper landed on top and jabbed her in the stomach as he did. That smacked the breath right out of her.

As she stared up at him, watching as he struggled to pin her, he could see – for the first time – doubt in her eyes. Between the two of them, he was the winner. Not her.

But Sariah wouldn't quit. It was then she screamed. A shrill, echoing sound which would grab attention from anyone passing her flat.

He jammed a palm over her mouth to stifle her noise. The other going for her throat to choke it out of her.

She shook her head, trying to force him to let go. Her wailing noise kept escaping, though muffled.

All his life he'd had idiots comment on the smallness of his hands. He had always told them they were perfectly in proportion with the rest of him. But compared to Sariah's vulgar mouth, they were far too petite. He tried to jam it shut, but she kept wriggling it free. Her screams kept coming.

The two cousins struggled on the floor. He had her arms pinned under his knees and, although she kicked her legs and tried to swivel her hips, he was too heavy for the emaciated bitch to knock to the floor. Still the screaming came. One hand squeezed her throat tighter, giving all he had; the other smothering her mouth, trying to shut her noise. It was then his little finger slipped between her lips and her teeth clamped around it.

Jasper cried out, reeling as her teeth sank into his skin. Her eyes were filled with utter malice – a carnivore who wanted to chew on his flesh like a dog toy. Grunting with exertion, he squeezed her throat even tighter, trying to make her blackout so she'd let him go. He was going to kill her, he'd known it since she walked in, but this trauma gave greater urgency. He needed to free his fucking finger!

The two of them glared at each other.

It was around the eyes one could see the familial relationship between these two very different people. Especially when both sets filled with murderous hatred.

There was one final muffled cry, a desperate last gasp from her, as he squeezed and pressed with all his strength.

Then there was a snap in her neck. A gratifying sound, if it wasn't for her jaw locking at the exact same moment.

With his own cry, Jasper rolled off her.

The bitch was dead!

But with her last flicker of life she had bit his little finger clean off.

And the severed digit was in her mouth!

CHAPTER EIGHT

Jasper rolled over on her lounge floor and tried not to squeal. No one welcomes the sight of their own blood, particularly when it's gushing from one's hand. His heart pounding, he tried to get clear in his head what had happened.

In those final few seconds, Jasper had felt how sharp another human being's teeth could be. He'd experienced them not only pierce the skin and sink through his flesh, but gnaw and snap at the bone beneath. It might have been imagination, but he would swear he'd felt the warmth of her saliva on the bone itself.

He shifted and as he did the blood sprayed upwards – some kind of bizarre ornamental fountain. With sweaty desperation, he smothered his wounded left hand in the sleeve of his jacket. Trying to staunch the flow. He didn't want to be found weakly unconscious beside her corpse.

Keeping his distance, he regarded her skinny, pale body. He'd heard the crack in her neck, but she could still be pretending to be deceased so she could launch a sneaky attack on him. That's the kind of underhand thing Sariah would do. (He had broken into her flat, but she was the real criminal.) A clock in the kitchen ticked by two minutes, the sound possessing a strange echoing emptiness. And when no fresh breath was taken, Jasper sighed with relief.

She was dead. Never again was Jasper going to see her smug pout or hear about her debauched antics. Sariah was dead and good riddance!

The pressing fucking problem though was she had his finger.

Stumbling to his feet, he knew he had to retrieve it. It was evidence of his culpability. There was also a chance doctors could reattach it if he got it to them quickly enough.

He knelt at her side. Holding his left hand close to his body, he reached with his right. Pulling back her sluttish lips, which remained warm. They gave a squelch of blood as they parted. And a small exhalation of air escaped and the sound made him a tremble from his core outwards. He almost curled into a ball at that instant, but held himself together. Just stale air caught in her dead lungs, he told himself, before slipping his fingers into the bloody darkness of her mouth. His skin shivered as he touched the cold enamel of her sharp teeth. Jasper steadied himself. Turning his hand to reach under them and prise them open.

Jesus Christ! It was well and truly locked.

With the snap of her neck, her jaw had sealed itself shut.

Jasper already knew the last few minutes of her life had been too noisy, but he couldn't help himself from letting go with a roar of frustration.

Her entire existence she had been a sharpened point jabbed through his flesh. That raison d'être clearly wasn't altering now she was dead. How could she be this much of a bitch to him?

He had to move fast. Achingly regaining his feet and doing his best not to lose too much more blood, he staggered to the kitchen and retrieved the crowbar.

It was a good sized piece of metal, but when he stood above her with it, he realised the most dreadful thing: he would have to use both hands to lever open her jaw.

Swallowing once, he reached his left hand from his jacket and sickness rose at how bad it looked. Tendons and nerves hung loose and frayed over his knuckle. This had to be done though.

He bit down as hard as he could on the inside of his cheeks, hoping to draw enough blood to distract from the pain. The handle of the crowbar felt unnaturally cold between his fingers, the wound rubbing against it, his nerve endings screaming against the hard steel.

However, he held it steady and slipped the tip between her lips.

Once more the two cousins locked gazes. He could see an echo of nastiness in her eyes, a reminder of her utter baseness as a human being.

Using all the force his shoulders and arms could muster, he levered the crowbar. There was another gigantic crack. Much louder than the bone in her neck. Her jaw flew open, along with the top half of her face. Suddenly her cheeks stretched so wide he thought her flesh had ripped.

Her mouth was a yawning, black chasm.

Ungainly he fell backwards. The jagged wound on his left hand not only striking the floor, but being crushed by his falling torso. The pain was incredible, his vision filled for a few seconds with a bright red. He cried out and then scrabbled around the carpet whimpering. When he finally stopped, he realised there was another sound:

A tap-tap-tap at her front door.

"Sariah!" a voice called.

Shit! Who the fuck was there?

The voice was young and male. A neighbour, or one of her many, many boyfriends. Either way, there was a genuine possibility he might have a key.

Jasper needed to be swift.

Crawling along the floor, he tried not to stare too much at the black void which dominated her face. Her jaw had gone from being sealed tight to completely dislocated. If he didn't know it was Sariah, he wouldn't have recognised her. Darkness had swallowed her features.

Turning as best he could because he couldn't bear to glimpse it, he shoved the fingers of his right hand in – slow and trembling, in case somehow her jaw slammed shut again and took more of his digits – and felt around to rescue his finger.

At the depths of his mind, he'd had the idea to burn the place to cinders. Muddy the crime scene. Make it harder for them. Destroy any DNA of his on the walls or carpet.

Whether he could do it with the chinless idiot outside, he didn't know. But if he could just retrieve his finger, then he could determine what to do next.

However, he couldn't find it. Jasper reached in there blindly and then, in sheer disbelief, propped himself up and stared into the disgusting hole which was her broken flesh.

His fucking finger wasn't there!

Not only had the bitch bitten it off, but in her very last action of life – because she never got sick of spiting him – she'd swallowed it.

Feeling light-headed and caught in utter disbelief, he nearly roared again.

"Sariah!" the voice cried more urgently from the front door. "Sariah!"

This made Jasper move. He grabbed the crowbar and scrambled to his feet.

The young man was getting panicky. It wouldn't be long before police were in this room.

There'd be DNA tests!

He was a law-abiding citizen; there was no record of him in any criminal database, but eventually they'd spot the familial relationship between killer and victim. After that, it wouldn't take much in the way of enquiries to pop around to Belinda's place.

Behind him, the tapping on the front door had become a pounding.

Jasper needed an injection of money if he was to flee the country before the investigation caught up with him. He doubted that, if he had time to search Sariah's flat, he'd find anything over fifty quid. The bitch had obviously spent all she'd got on booze and cocaine.

This left the Fallowford bastard Trust – whatever they were!

They had his money and by all which was righteous, they would place it in his hands. The time for being delicate was over, from this point on he would embrace recklessness.

"Sariah!" the voice called, as Jasper disappeared out the back door.

CHAPTER NINE

The night before, not long after Breakspear's departure, Simone had left the casino alone. The champagne was consumed, so what was the point of hanging around? It would only be to bat away passes from unattractive men. And all men at quarter past eleven at night, with a few drinks inside them, are remarkably unattractive.

She told Robin they should return to the hotel room, but he replied he was fine. A smile on his face, he suggested she go and enjoy herself. Lord knows what he was up to. His great prospect had been shot down and normally this pissed him off, but tonight he was almost phlegmatic. She knew Belinda Daindridge hadn't responded to the call he'd made earlier that afternoon, but maybe he had a different girlfriend lined up. If it was another prospect he hadn't mentioned it, which would be strange. Maybe this was someone he'd just met. Good for him, if the case.

It was his decision and she never argued with him when he said he'd be okay. It might have been odd for adult siblings to share the same room, but it was distinctly unhealthy for them to never spend a night away from each other.

Robin had had bad dreams for a long time. Too many years. And when they came, she was the only one who could soothe him. She had tried to get him to commit to therapy, but it required more effort than he would give. Her brother was one of the most wonderful, caring men she knew, but he was also flighty and preferred to run. Their occupation meant they frequently had to disappear hurriedly and thus it suited him fine.

That night, after a quick text exchange, she got a cab to the house of her new friend, Lizzie. Lizzie was a trainee teacher with huge, curly, jet-black hair, a beautiful round face, a nice bust, a round arse and an absolute cackle of a laugh. Although they'd met in a gay bar and Lizzie had made it clear quickly (if clumsily) over martinis that she was interested, she still wasn't confident about her sexuality. She'd been drunk that night, drunk enough to allow herself to be talked into going to a gay bar – in bright lipstick and a low-cut top – but mostly she was circumspect. As if she didn't reside in London in the twenty-first century.

Lizzie lived alone and it was dark when Simone arrived, but still she dragged Simone through the door before any of the neighbours could get a glimpse of her. Perhaps imagining the young teacher in her pyjama shorts welcoming a glamorous lady in a red dress after dark would scandalise them.

"You must excuse me," Lizzie said, bustling around the kitchen and making them both a cup of tea. As nervous as a first date. "It's been a hell of a day and a busy night, I might need to sleep. I do want you here," she added, worried in case Simone imagined she was inviting her to leave, "but I need to sleep tonight, if that's okay."

It was. And to prove it, Simone took Lizzie in her arms and hugged her, to calm her and make her feel safe. But once they were in each other's grasp, all thoughts of a nice cup of tea were forgotten. One thing led to another and they were panting on the bed when they heard midnight chime from a nearby church tower.

"You were with your brother tonight then?" Lizzie asked, as they cuddled together afterwards.

Simone nodded.

"It's great you guys are close. I mean, I'm close to my brother, but we only speak once a fortnight. We text a lot, but it's not the same."

Close wasn't strong enough a word for what had built up between her and Robin, Simone thought. 'Dependency' would have been more appropriate.

"We've been through a lot."

She could sense Lizzie thinking about it, but she must have decided she and Simone weren't close enough yet to venture into those waters.

Instead Lizzie asked: "What's he doing tonight?"

"I don't know. He could be working, or maybe he has his own assignation." They both giggled a little at the word. "He doesn't like to go to sleep in a bedroom alone."

"Are any of his girlfriends cute?"

Simone laughed. "He has a thing for the older woman, shall we say?"

"Really?"

"Yes. He has issues to work through."

To put it mildly.

They both giggled.

"Can I ask you a question?" Lizzie said, after another pause.

"Sure."

"What is it you do?"

"We run a charitable trust and also have investment portfolios," she said. Although maybe too quickly. To her ears then it sounded what it was: a rote answer, vague enough to mean anything.

Lizzie nodded and ran her fingers across Simone's naked stomach "I like you," she said.

In the dim light, Simone peered into the younger woman's bright eyes. "I like you too."

"But it seems to me, well, you live in a hotel room, you have a job which – I don't understand what it is, but sounds to me you could do it anywhere. And – not that there's anything wrong with this – your brother is the most important person in your life. From what I know so far" – she hunted for the right phrase – "you don't seem to have any permanency. You and your brother could disappear any day and I'd never hear from you."

"What are you saying?" Simone shifted a little, but didn't move out of Lizzie's arms.

"I'm saying I like you. I really like you. And I don't want you to disappear on me."

Simone leant in and kissed her full on the lips. "I will do my absolute best not to disappear on you."

They both laughed once more. In the quiet intimacy between them it sounded a joke. Simone tried not to dwell on the fact it was the most reassurance she could offer.

CHAPTER TEN

In the dank, dark master bedroom of Breakspear Hall, pale sunlight crept through the naked window. There was no way for Montagu Breakspear to tell anymore if it was sunset or dawn. Every shade of hour was agony within those walls. Clocks ticked, but time was meaningless.

He sat at the edge of his bed, wearing a stained and torn grey vest and underpants. Confusion creased into his brow as he examined his arms and legs. He couldn't remember what had happened to them, but there were thick rivulets of blood running in parallel across both.

Long ago he'd lost track of what were his nightmares and what was his reality. He had come to the realisation there was negligible difference between the two. All the tortures blurred together. He had no accurate recollection of what had happened to him, but his wounds said they had forced him into the positon of a supplicant. In the darkness they had placed him on his knees, his hands opened outwards, his forearms pressed to the side of his thighs. Then someone – or something – had whipped him. A thick lash slicing into his exposed flesh. Distantly he could hear the swish of air which ended with a crack and his own howl of pain.

No, not pain. He told himself he had moved beyond pain.

The only grace he'd found in shutting off from the fake pleasure the house offered him was, as time passed, he was also closed down to the pain. These walls could try their most diabolical methods and he would scarcely flinch

There were other new lesions. An instrument with spikes had been used to beat him. Across his legs and arms, there were also small puncture wounds. He could only imagine an implement where sharp nails pointed out in concentric circles. Blood had bubbled from the dozens of small holes and congealed into vivid patterns.

There had been so much of it in his life, he was immune now to the terror. All he felt in the thin light was numb confusion.

Only one thing in Breakspear Hall – not the beatings, nor the abuse, nor the way the very brickwork became cruel faces and screamed at him – could raise alarm in his breast. That was when Murkiss approached him.

The butler whom he had inherited with the house.

With a shudder, Breakspear realised the man stood above him.

"Now, sir," the butler's mild tone said. "I do hate to be an awful nag, but I'm afraid I will have to insist – as much as I can – that you go out. It's no good you sitting around the house by yourself. You must engage with the world, you have to meet someone. This house has given you wonderful years, but it's time to think of the future."

Wonderful years? Was that what he was calling it?

Murkiss was a moon faced individual. Bald, apart from tufts of hair to the side of his head, which he seemed to have grown out so they were neat shelves above his ears; his bland, chinless face indicated an unassuming sort used to fading into the background. His liveries were always spotless – no matter what liquids spilled or gushed from elsewhere in the house – suggesting a man who took vain pride-in his work. Good at his job. A person without ego who had embraced his inconsequence in life. But Breakspear had long peered behind the mask of this man – or creature or demon, or whatever he was – and knew that under his hooded, deep seated eyes burned a hate-filled fire. The portly frame, the hands behind the back, the harmless set of his features, were a disguise for unadulterated darkness.

The first time he had arrived at Breakspear Hall as the new owner – painfully long ago now – Murkiss had swung open the door and welcomed him over the threshold. Informed him he was proud to consider Mr Breakspear his new master. It didn't take long for Breakspear to realise the power lay in the other direction. Even when it was only the two of them, pretence was made. In outward appearance, Murkiss seemed utterly deferential.

"We have deduced what you are thinking, sir, and I'm afraid you are mistaken if you consider your scheme will be a success." Murkiss shook his head more in sadness than anger. "You think you can die here without heir and it will bring everything to a halt. Isn't that right, sir? But whereas it's true you are an old man – if you don't mind me saying, sir – and it is not possible for the rejuvenating properties of this magnificent house to keep you alive forever, your plan is simply misguided."

He stepped forward and coughed once, preparing to broach a subject of the utmost delicacy. "Sir," when he spoke, his voice – for all its inherent politeness – had gained a nasty edge. "The fact is you may very well die in this house and you may die alone. But please understand, your death – for you – will not be soon and it will not be painless. We will make you suffer for every minute. Hours will be months and the days will be years. You can try this plan if you desire, sir, but I guarantee you will not get far into it before you are crying out that we are right and you need to venture into the world. Eventually, sooner than you think, you will see our point of view and let me drive you into town in the Rolls. Simply to save yourself the agonies.

"There may be a determination within you to resist what we inflict. And, I must say, sir, your tolerance is most impressive. But we will reach you. We will twist you around and break you if we have to. And through it all, we will make sure you live. We will guarantee you are breathing and feeling – truly feeling – it all."

He smiled, his tone softening and becoming what passed as friendly. "Why don't you be a good man and save yourself the torment? Why not go see who you can meet? Make a friend, sir."

Trembling on the bed, Breakspear shook his head. His mouth made the words: "No, I can't," but no sound emerged.

Without moving, the butler seemed to have drawn closer. Barely leaving an inch between them. "Your father paid for an excellent education, sir. He made sure you had the best advantages. So please put on your suit, do your hair and daub yourself with some of your expensively purchased charm. Otherwise…"

The words trailed off. The butler's voice replaced by a thousand screams, each of them clawing their way through Breakspear's ears and into the shrivelled husk of his quaking soul.

CHAPTER ELEVEN

"What do you think?" asked Robin.

This wasn't best practice, or whatever term they would use for best practice in their line of work. They were in the same venue as last night, but now they were considering the second target Robin had discussed.

"I don't like it," Simone muttered from the corner of her mouth. Lips barely moving.

They were being subtle. She was resting at the bar, having ordered a virgin cocktail which she contemplated with an intensity that suggested it contained all the world's booze and could quell the pain of a million heartaches. Robin was to her left, a pillar stood between them, appearing louche and regarding his fellow gamblers with casual disinterest. A lounge lizard in training, ready to put the moves on an unsuspecting lady, or perhaps gentleman.

"He's good for it," he told her. "Worth a lot too."

"He was number two last night, darling. What makes him suddenly good enough for all our attentions?"

"We've got to work, darling." Robin took a sip of his whisky sour and grinned at a tall, dapper man going past. Probably giving him the wrong impression. "And this is a good target. Just one which comes with a much tighter time limit than old Breakspear."

Did they have to work? Wasn't their bank balance filled quite nicely? From his end, Belinda Daindridge's last cheque was still lovely and warm. While for her, it was only a few weeks since she let down that old racist fart, Datchett. Couldn't they take time off? There was a five star holiday resort a friend of hers had recommended in Costa Rica. Couldn't they go there for a few weeks?

Robin never wanted to holiday. He said he did, but he didn't. When they took a break, it was never for long. There was always the next job and the one after and the one after. It would not matter how big their bank accounts grew, they'd keep going.

To humour her brother, she glanced over her shoulder at the latest target. Testing whether her profile and a raised eyebrow would be enough to tempt him.

The man was an American cowboy in London. Rangy, broad shouldered, with a long face lined by too much sun. He had dyed black hair and a dyed black moustache, and he was with friends – or men he was choosing to call friends for an evening – and laughing in a deep rumble.

What she gave him was nothing like her best come hither look, but it wasn't inconsequential either. He didn't notice. Too lost in impressing his dudes.

"What did he do again?" she asked.

"Embezzlement. Pension fund. Cleared after an investigation. Although the state governor is a golfing buddy."

"It's probably more cut and dried than the old man from last night, darling."

"Yes, but tick-tock. We only have a week before his return flight. You will have to really get into him to make him give a shit about the poor orphans of Fallowford."

Simone took a big gulp of her pineapple juice, cranberry juice and lemonade all mixed together and wished the barman had snuck a large shot of vodka in there. She sighed. "You make the decisions, remember?"

"Please, it's a partnership. We're partners. We're a team. An exceptional team!"

She rolled her eyes. "Why are we really here? Do you genuinely want this one, or are you hoping Breakspear will show tonight and you'll have a second chance?"

He didn't answer her for a minute. Someone who might have been an acquaintance went past and instead Robin shook his hand and wished him the best for the night's gambling. When he came back to her, after ordering another drink, he said:

"Well, he'll recognise us and, you're right, he must have been intrigued. The chance exists his curiosity would get the better of him."

"And the notoriety of a murder case appeals to you, doesn't it?"

"That and the fact the man has clearly been enjoying his nice, big house all these years after his empty promises."

She sighed. "But he hasn't shown, has he?"

"No."

"And thus you want us to take Tex? What's he into?

Boys or girls?"

"Oh, you're very much his type, darling!" Robin said, almost loud enough to be overheard. "But then so is anything in a skirt."

Again she glanced at the cowboy. A long way from Houston, but in a denim shirt with a shoelace tie. He was laughing so hard at his own jokes, he was actually slapping his thigh.

She shuddered and finished her drink. Promising herself the next one would be a double something, or she'd never make it through the night.

"We'll have to wait for him to leave his friends," she said.

"Of course."

"While I'm waiting I'm going to get a cigarette. Maybe when I return, if he's alone. I'll think of an inspired way to make an introduction."

She made her way through the bar. Tonight she was in a more casual and shorter forest green dress. One with a high neckline, bare arms and a loose, pleated skirt which stopped just above her knees. She didn't pay attention to whether Tex checked her out as she went past, although she was sure Robin was gauging his every reaction.

No, she was thinking of Lizzie the night before. Somehow conning a visiting cowboy didn't seem the kind of thing which would lend permanency to one's life. They'd be running again soon, she could feel it and she was dreading it.

She took the lift, stepped into the chilly evening air, retrieving her cigarette case and her lighter from her clutch handbag. They were young, Robin always said, they had plenty of time to worry about the future. But standing under the streetlamp, she couldn't recall the last time she'd felt quite so glum. How was all this going to end?

CHAPTER TWELVE

Across the road, in the darkness of his car, Jasper Redditch sat and watched.

He had got across London and to his tidy house in Woolwich without further accident. Obviously there was the genuine worry he'd lose so much blood he'd pass out behind the wheel at a traffic light, but driving slowly and one handed, he managed the whole journey.

Once inside, with the door locked behind him, he'd fashioned a bandage which covered the ragged hole where his little finger should be. It pinched into the flesh of his hand and, although excruciatingly painful, stopped the dribbling of blood.

However, as a remedy, it was a long journey from perfect. In the hours since, he'd had to change the dressing twice when it became too soaked. But it was a constant seeping, rather than a spurting, so at least he could function. What it needed was stitches, but he couldn't go to the hospital as there'd be too many questions. And he was a law-abiding citizen, not a man who would know where to find one of those criminal doctors who appear conveniently in movies.

(On the silver screen they often seemed to be vets. But he couldn't imagine ringing the doorbell of his local establishment and asking if they'd take a look at it right after they'd dealt with a sick Chihuahua.)

No, the only way he could get it tended, it seemed to him, was to go abroad and find a doctor who wouldn't ask too many questions. For that he would need money.

Belinda had none he could access. Sariah certainly had none. Which left The Fallowford Trust.

Once in his house, despite the shock and the blood loss and his sheer rage at how Sariah could do this to him, he logged onto his PC and discovered all he could about this supposed charity.

There were two directors: a brother and a sister.

When he searched for an address for them however, there was no luck. They didn't seem to have a full-time residence. The charity itself was registered at a solicitor's office in Bournemouth, so it was no help whatsoever. But Jasper was a man with resources. His job had been at the high-end of credit checks. Not the standard type where some lobotomised desk jockey typed the details into a computer and waited for it to decide yes or no. He could train any baboon to do that. No, where he'd made his living required more expert deduction.

That afternoon he had called one of his former colleagues. A man he was still on good terms with, despite the unpleasantness which had caused him to quit. After enquiring after this bloke's chubby wife and chubbier child, he'd got him to run a proper search on both brother and sister. It seemed a credit card belonging to the brother had been used to check into

The Regal Hotel on Park Lane two days ago.

One twin room for the two of them? It didn't sit right with Jasper.

In fact, nothing he learned of the siblings made him feel easy they were worthy custodians of his money. It took a bit of hunting, but he located a few photos of them online. They didn't seem charitable types to him. No, they were beautiful people. And if there was one thing he'd learned about beautiful people, it was that they only cared for themselves.

More digging brought him an old news story concerning the brother and what a wretch of a human being he was. This solidified the contempt in his mind.

Jasper shook his head. What the hell was Belinda playing at giving money to these people? Did she do no research at all? Well, it was his money and they would return every damn penny. There was no question of it.

Alone in his bathroom, he arranged it so a glove squeezed against the top of his bandage. It hurt like damnation, as those leather driving gloves were tight to begin with, but it made the wound pretty much invisible to anyone who looked at him. Plus, he hoped the tightness would staunch the flow to pretty much nothing.

Then he headed to The Regal Hotel and waited.

It hadn't taken long. Nine o'clock, the two of them walked out. Both of them done up gleaming and glamorous. He darkly suspected they were heading to a party. Obviously Belinda had known them, but he wondered if Sariah had as well. They appeared to be the kind of venal, self-centred filth she'd have got along with.

An immaculate doorman beamed at them as he

opened the rear door of a black cab and ushered them in.

Then Jasper followed.

But where they went was far worse than any party of his imaginings. They took themselves to a casino. Some hidden, but exclusive place, off Piccadilly. The two of them were gambling with Belinda's money. Spinning the wheel on what should rightfully be his.

The venom he had felt for Sariah transferred to this poisonous pair.

A search on his phone told him it was a private members' club, with an 'introduction fee' which was obscenely ridiculous to a moral man like Jasper. It meant he couldn't just walk in there and yank the chips from their hands. Berate them in front of everyone for the scum they were.

Who knew when they would come out? Or how much cash they would lose in the meantime?

He had to sit in the cold and dark, thinking of them laughing as they threw dice and turned cards. With every passing second, the piles of money in his head diminishing.

But then, across the road, exiting the club by herself, was the bitch of a sister. She walked down the street a couple of doors, stood at the corner under a lamp, then lit herself a cigarette. If he had to guess, he'd say she didn't want to be bothered by those going in and out of the club. There'd be all those hands to shake and cheeks to kiss and she no doubt wanted somewhere to smoke in peace. (And maybe it wasn't even tobacco. He could well believe that of her.) The woman looked to be in a ruminative mood, and he hoped to God that meant she hadn't lost too much of his money.

Well, she would not lose any fucking more.

He opened his car door, stepped out and shut it softly behind him.

The beautiful people consider themselves immune to the problems of the everyday. There's always someone to do them a favour. An old friend who could lend them a luxury yacht if they had nowhere to go. They didn't understand that for normal and decent people – Jasper Redditch, for one – life could be hard and debts would mount and everything became a struggle. It would infuriate him enough if it was her own money this bitch was throwing around. But the fact it was his was abominable.

It would not do!

CHAPTER THIRTEEN

Even conscious of the autumn chill, Simone was considering not re-entering the warm casino. Instead she could call Lizzie and stay with her until Robin decided on a proper target. The prospect of nights alone would make him focus.

A guilty smile rose to her lips when she contemplated the good chance that Lizzie wouldn't answer. Theirs had been such a late night, it was dawn when they'd dropped off. The poor love was shattered even before a day of looking after little ones. She'd more than likely be asleep, but you never knew. There was an attachment between them and Simone was sure Lizzie would be delighted to offer her a place to stay. Even if Simone had to wake her.

What was the alternative?

That bloody cowboy?

The thought riddled her with dread. His hand on her arse as she tried to ward off his tongue later tonight. Having to pretend to be sexually available, pushing hard and fast over the next week so he'd hand them a substantial cheque by the end of it.

And then what?

Another old man? Another middle-aged lady?

Eventually they would have to change cities as they'd have run things dry in London, but globally Robin seemed to have to tapped an inexhaustible supply of these people. There was always another and another and another. Until what? Well, their youth would disappear one day. Already – at nearly thirty years old – Simone saw the occasional much younger woman, pheromones firing in all directions, wearing a tiny skirt and on the hunt for a much richer, older husband. There was no way Simone could compete with one of those.

Simone never slept with any of them. From the very start of it all, when she was less experienced and it was harder to fix the boundaries, she never gave in and went to bed with a single one. Robin did, of course he did. He took them all to bed. It was his job and his hobby.

For her, well, she was a gay woman who would turn thirty in four months' time. Many years ago she had dropped out of university for personal reasons, but she was bright and could go and study if she wanted. She still had the opportunity to do a lot with her life. But for now she was stuck on her brother's seemingly endless quest. One which, as much as he didn't want it to, would have a play to a conclusion eventually.

Last night Lizzie had been right. There was no permanency in her life. She dreamt of settling down, or having a wife and kids maybe. But how was she possibly going to do that when her job – her actual occupation – was to drape herself over seedy older men with dodgy histories and hope she could con money from them?

There was no way she could keep living like this. She wanted her life to have meaning.

Sighing with her shoulders, she stamped the cigarette under her heel and opened the case for another. It occurred to her that Lizzie might not know she smoked. Simone hadn't lit up when she was with her. Mainly because the one time they had been out together, they'd left the bar quickly. While their second date was an intimate candlelit dinner at Lizzie's place. Simone didn't smoke much and could quit anytime (or told herself so), but she reflected that if she was going to call Lizzie tonight, it would be courteous to dab on fresh perfume and have a mint in the cab on the way over.

"Excuse me!" a high pitched and agitated male voice called.

From across the road, a short, bald, ugly man was approaching her. He was almost defiantly unattractive, wearing brown ill cut trousers and a beige anorak which was functional at best. He looked pale, ill and sweaty, but what stood out was the sheer anger of the man. A storm of hate was bubbling off every inch of him. He was a terrible destructive weapon which, for some reason she could not fathom, was aimed directly at her.

"Excuse me!" he yelled again. "I'm correct in thinking I'm addressing Simone, aren't I?"

She closed her cigarette case and regarded him with amazement. How could he know her name? When in life would their paths have crossed?

"Excuse me!" he repeated for a third time. "What have you done with Belinda Daindridge's money?"

Her face revealed nothing. She was damn sure of

it. Simone straightened her shoulders and fixed him with a baffled gaze. Zero to hide, not sure what was going on.

"I don't know what you're talking about." Simone was as haughty and dismissive as she could be. Conscious if she was to turn and walk towards the club without a word, this furious little man would no doubt claim he wasn't responsible for what came next.

"You're The Fallowford Trust, aren't you?" His voice wasn't nasal, more a sound dredged from the back of the throat.

It wouldn't be wise for her to deny a fact easy to prove. "Yes."

"Well then, Belinda Daindridge has written you cheques for more than a quarter of a million pounds. That fact slipped your mind, has it?"

"Please, Mr..." she fished, but he didn't give her a name. "We have a lot of donors. I can't be expected to keep track of all of them."

He sneered, standing so close she caught a stomach-churning whiff of his B.O.. "A little charity, which no one has ever pigging heard of, gets a lot of huge donations , does it? Come on, do you think I'm stupid?"

She shook her head. "I would need to speak to our accountant. Or our solicitor."

"Mr Burbank?" he asked. "I bet you he's utterly bent, isn't he?"

The fact he knew their lawyer's name alarmed her. What else did he know? Already she understood this wasn't a lunatic from the street, but a man who had prepared.

She took a step from him and glanced to the casino door. The bouncer seemed to have disappeared. Where the hell was he? She looked over her shoulder, trying to spot him and saw an old fashioned Rolls-Royce pull up like a vision of death.

"Is your brother the one behind it?" the man snarled. "He's in there isn't he? Gambling with money which isn't his!"

"Please, Mr…"

He cut her off. Holding up a begloved hand which somehow seemed deformed.

"Save it!" he barked. "I want my fucking money or I'm going to the police!"

Simone shook her head, uncomprehending rather than saying no. "And you are?"

"I'm the man who will unload twenty tonnes of shit onto your pretty head if you don't. Do you want that, ay? Your entire face, body and tits covered in shit?"

The two of them glared at each other. Simone doing her best not to show any fear. An extraordinary feat when it was impossible to overestimate how deranged this horrid little man appeared.

She was distressingly aware how dark it was and, with the bouncer having slipped off doubtless to relieve himself, how utterly alone she was. There was only the Rolls and the thought was mad, but to her it (unwelcomingly) brought to mind her own hearse.

Undoubtedly she couldn't stay there. She had to move, run if she had to, scream at the top of her lungs if needs be.

"I think you need to send a letter to Mr Burbank," she said stiffly. "He will listen to any complaint you might have."

Simone turned on her heel, intent on racing down the road, but the man was faster than her. Before she'd got half a step, he'd grabbed her arm. She swung round, ready to hit him with her bag and then her heart plummeted as she caught the glint of a kitchen knife thrusting towards her.

CHAPTER FOURTEEN

The stuck-up bitch was just as strong as she looked. Up close she was the athletic type, despite her pretty frock. Never trust a woman with biceps, that was a truth and a half.

He had no intention of stabbing her right here on the street. That would be insane! How would he get his money then? But he could frighten her. More than frighten her, perhaps. Wound her a little and let her know how serious he was. Open a hole in that pretty dress of hers and draw a bead of blood. Something to command her respect. She'd stop struggling then.

But this one had pluck, much more than Belinda. (Hopefully though not quite as much as Sariah.) Her being taller than him gave her an unfair advantage. But he was a desperate man. He had suffered the slings and arrows of crappy fortune for too long and couldn't afford to take "no" for an answer anymore. The fact he wouldn't quit gave him the ultimate advantage.

Like a bull he charged in headfirst, the blade only a little bit behind. She arched herself from him and slammed her small, leather bag at his knife-hand and in the same movement grabbed at his head. For the first time in a while he appreciated the natural greasiness of his scalp as she struggled to get a grip on him. Too much of a lady to do what Sariah did and scratch into his flesh. Besides she didn't have the talons of that trollop.

She contorted herself as his thrusting knife arm got within millimetres of her. She backed against the nearest wall, the fear all too obvious in her eyes. It obliterated her smugness and confidence. She feared she would die tonight. Good! Let her keep that dread in mind.

No one had come past yet. There were no moving cars and the big, bald bouncer he'd spotted earlier was AWOL. But Jasper's luck would not last long. He had to quell her, make her see reason. His arm jabbed forward again and she flinched, moving sideways. The tip of the blade whistled as it slit open a hole in the front of her dress, almost giving her a spectacularly wide navel.

She screamed. Until then she hadn't given vent to her fear, but now she shrieked. From deep in her lungs, a sound which filled the entire street. He'd been expecting it, he'd seen her mouth open and known it was coming, but the fury of it made him jump.

Although it didn't stop him.

The police had already been to Sariah's place, they may already have found Belinda. They'd be keen to speak to him as the only remaining family member. This evening he had to get ahead of them, and this bitch was the key. She had lots of money and could easily afford to give him Belinda's squandered pounds so he could be on his way.

Why wouldn't she stop her selfishness and hand him what was rightfully his?

Surprise was the thing. It hurt to hell, but he punched with his left hand. Aiming to cuff her in the jaw and stop the yelling, but instead he smacked into her collar-bone. Jesus! Red splotches appeared in front of his eyes and there was a fraction of a second of wooziness, but then he felt a kind of triumph. It hadn't been as hard as he could have hit with his right, but it had been enough. The blow had knocked her off balance and she dropped her bag and fell. Hit her arse on the pavement, her legs splayed wide, giving him a glimpse of black lacy knickers. Now she was staring at him wide-eyed. The terror on her face was truly gratifying and almost eased the pain in his left hand.

He spat to the floor, resembling an uncouth teenager, and hoped the taste of blood on his lips was merely a hallucination.

His mouth opened and he was about to tell her she had to come with him. That he wouldn't hurt her as long as she went to her bank first thing in the morning and withdrew all the money he wanted.

But instead, he heard a voice behind him. Deep and utterly unexpected.

"What is going on here?"

The surprise spun Jasper around. He feared an attack and thrust the blade, slitting open the old man's guts.

CHAPTER FIFTEEN

Scrabbling to her knees, Simone recognised Breakspear at once. Cold air brushed against her bare midriff. She pulled the torn clothing tight with trembling hands and slowly pushed herself forward to her knees. Ready to jump.

After giving an animal roar of frustration, the short, ugly, bald man's mouth opened and closed helplessly. At first it seemed his feet wouldn't move. He was an ominous statue. Knife dripping red in his hand, he gawped at Breakspear's collapsed, bleeding form with utter incomprehension. Then he turned his gaze to her and she could see his fevered mind trying to formulate a response. She thought he would reach his begloved hand to her. Finish what he'd begun while Breakspear bled to death behind them.

But then, she unfroze and screamed at the top of her lungs and he got the message.

The man could try and wrestle with her. However, someone else was most bound to get there soon, and the ugly little git didn't want to be present when they did.

So he ran across the road. He may have wanted money, but now she guessed venal cowardice and self-preservation took over and he disappeared into the darkness. Peering shocked at the pale, dying form of Breakspear, she vaguely heard a past-its-prime car engine fail to start the first time, before engaging and roaring away.

Breakspear lay on the pavement, his hands crossed over the gaping wound of his belly. She solicitously clutched onto them, her own fingers trembling as she felt the coldness of his flesh. Hoping between the two of them they could staunch the bleeding, but knowing deep within it was hopeless.

Where had he come from?

A large selfish part of her was glad he'd shown up, as it meant the knife hadn't stuck into her. His arrival had saved her, but she didn't want anything to happen to him as a consequence. He could have frightened away the little creep without having his insides torn apart. Yet instead here he was, an old man bleeding on the street. An old man with a poor reputation who had saved her life.

Sobs trembled her entire body. Her jaw opening and closing, but with no idea what words of thanks or sympathy to use. Helpless she crouched over his greying face. He looked old. Really old. His skin was creased with pained lines and was pale to the point of translucence. The blood was pumping from his stomach, creating a sheen across the paving stones. At first she gave a gasp of relief when the flow seemed to ease, but then she realised what it meant. His heart was stopping. He was dying in front of her. This man had stepped in to save her and he was going to perish for it.

Suddenly there was movement at her shoulder and Robin was there. He had, across the years, done various first aid courses. He was stronger than her and he pressed down tighter and in a better position. It still wasn't going to do any good.

"What the hell happened?" His voice was high, shaky.

She was so stunned she replied with her own question. "What are you doing here?"

"I came to cadge a cigarette. Si. Tell me what happened."

"Some man," she said, not able to comprehend it. "He had a knife."

Robin could have guessed that much, but didn't press further. "In my pocket," he said. "There's my phone. Call 999."

She'd had her own phone in her bag, but it had dropped to the ground in the struggle and she hadn't thought of it. Her blood stained fingers reached into his trouser pocket and managed at the third attempt to retrieve his mobile. Her red fingerprints smeared across the screen.

But before she had a chance to dial the emergency number, a car pulled up in front of them.

It was that Silver Ghost Rolls-Royce. Without her noticing, it must have performed a three point turn and now faced away from the casino. It was a vision. The notion striking her ridiculously it was the kind of car a 1920s gentleman detective drove around in.

Simone and Robin gazed up hopefully, but fearfully. What else could this evening hold?

The man who stepped out seemed to be composed of moonlight. That distant blue light sheathed his skin as he moved around from the driver's side. He was a moon faced man in an old fashioned butler's uniform. Not fast on his feet, but he stood before them with his hands spread from his side, eager to be of assistance.

"Please." His voice was an urgent whisper. "I am Mr Breakspear's man, Murkiss. If you place him in the car, I can get him home and look after him."

"Home?" Robin was aghast. "This man needs a hospital!"

Murkiss coughed and raised his hand politely to his plump lips. "Mr Breakspear has various underlying conditions which a hospital may take time to get to grips with. Too much time, I fear. I feel he will do better at home."

The sight of the butler seemed to imbue Breakspear with more strength. He was breathless and feeble, yet forced himself up a little on one elbow. "No!" he grunted through the pain. "Hospital!"

"What?" Robin exclaimed. "That's insane!"

Simone agreed. "I think he needs to go to the hospital. They can look after him."

"Are you a medical man yourself, sir?" asked Murkiss.

Robin shook his head, pressing tight to Breakspear's stomach. "No, I'm not. But I'm…"

The butler didn't let him finish. "I see you have a good idea of what you are doing. That you understand first-aid techniques. Perhaps you could help me put Mr Breakspear into the back of the car. We will head toward home, but I will take your judgement. If you feel at any point a hospital will better serve him, then I will divert the vehicle."

"No!" Breakspear yelled again.

Simone thought he was going to say 'hospital' next,

but wasn't sure.

"I think he needs a hospital."

"There's no reason to waste seconds arguing on the subject, sir. An ambulance will take a good few minutes to get here. Time, I fear, Mr Breakspear doesn't have. We should get going."

The butler was already reaching under Montagu Breakspear, lifting the tall man's shoulders, but looking to Robin for help. After only a moment's more debate with himself, her brother gave in. The two of them carried him with a lack of strain; she could almost believe Breakspear was balsa and felt stitched together.

For a few seconds, Simone stayed crouched on the pavement, a hand across her bare stomach. She watched them without movement. Wondering if she should remain behind and alert the police there was a maniac on the loose. Pondering whether, absurd as it sounded, she should let them go and follow along in a black cab.

Then Robin glanced at her, his eyebrow raised, a question on his face: why the hell wasn't she with him?

Catching her breath, she retrieved her clutch-bag and forced herself to totter to the open door. Seemingly a woman who'd never worn heels before.

"As you wish, Miss." Murkiss said, as she climbed in with her brother. The man closed the door behind them.

Her gaze flitted to the street, to the pool of blood which would have the police poring over security footage later. When she was a child she'd often got car sick and the memory of the sensation returned abruptly. There was something not right about this. They had to help Breakspear but she felt there was something utterly wrong about what was happening.

The man was gravely injured, yet the way he groaned didn't resemble pain any more. He lay across from them and Robin continued to press tight to the wound. However, when her eyes caught the old man's, she saw they were fearful beyond comprehension. It was a dread which bled into her. As the vintage car pulled off smoothly, she wished that – despite the fact Montagu Breakspear had no doubt saved her life and she owed him – she could have remained on the pavement.

CHAPTER SIXTEEN

The first time she saw Breakspear Hall – the building which would come to haunt every one of her nightmares – Simone gasped.

Matters were already tense in the car. As soon as they'd turned the first corner, Robin demanded a hospital. But Murkiss, calm and unperturbed in the front seat, ignored him. A pane of polished glass stood between him and the chauffeured passengers, and the man had driven across the Thames and towards South East London without a glance back. Even though she could only see the back of his head, there were times she thought he was about to whistle a merry tune. The only thing which stopped Robin yelling, or trying to open the door at any traffic lights they came to, was that now they were in the car Breakspear did – against every expectation – seem to improve. The blood seepage was easing, but not in the frightening way she'd witnessed on the pavement. And colour was returning to his face. The old man didn't look healthy, but he wasn't snuggling next to death.

Maybe this butler was right and his home did have strange recuperative qualities. But how could such a thing be possible?

They sailed through areas of London she'd never seen before. Past terraced and semi-detached houses and thousands of families asleep at this late hour of the night. The normal world she'd never been part of and which seemed to be slipping further by the mile. Then they turned and left it all behind. At a sharp bend, the car exited a pleasant, unassuming road for a long, tree lined driveway. The moon only a faint glow above the overgrown trees. Blackthorns she thought they were. At the top of this narrow one track private road, which must have been a mile along, stood Breakspear Hall.

It was a large, imposing, gothic house. Standing grey and indomitable and lit a ghostly blue by the clear night sky.

Simone guessed it was some kind of Victorian folly. An industrial age businessman building his dream home and not realising how scary his romantic fantasy would appear. It was grey stone, had a tower and turrets at each end, an immense oak door (twice the size of an average human being) and various arched windows crossed with bars. Outside, over the years of its existence, a wild, creeping vine had been allowed to grow to gigantic proportions. Against the brickwork this vegetation shone almost purple, giving the impression of disease on top of ghostliness.

The building stood alone on a small hill, the grounds around it empty apart from wild trees and bushes. She knew the suburbs weren't far back, yet it felt they were cut off from them. Unnaturally away from everyone else. Isolated.

Simone wasn't superstitious, she wasn't easily

alarmed. But at first glance, having been harassed on the street and witnessed what happened to Breakspear and with his blood spread over her clothes, the first sight of the structure rendered her speechless. It didn't feel welcoming. It was the opposite of welcoming. The entire edifice there to alienate her, to push her away. Her first response on seeing Breakspear Hall was that she didn't want to go in and, as crazy as it might sound, she imagined the building reciprocated the feeling. It would delight the house not to have her darken its doors.

Her brother however, didn't seem to give a second glance to this grey monstrosity of purple-veined bricks rising out of the hill. But then he was on his knees in the back of the car, trying to close the wound with his bare hands. If he was surprised by the colour returning to Breakspear's cheeks, or the fearful alertness which shone now in the old man's eyes, he didn't show it. All he knew was there was an injured man in front of him, a life his training could save, and he would try his best.

Robin's phone reception had died in the car. She'd been checking it the whole journey. They were at the centre of one of the world's major cities, but there was nothing at all. In panic, she'd grabbed hers from her clutch-bag and it was the same story.

"It's okay, old man." Robin spoke fast, his adrenaline pumping. "You've got a landline, right? We'll call 999 and get you seen to. You're looking much better, but I think you need a doctor to examine you. But we'll get it sorted. Don't give up hope."

Breakspear gritted his teeth and fixed furious eyes on him. The old man did appear much stronger, but it was impossible to disregard how much pain he was in. It was also hard to ignore that behind the fury, lurked something close to terror.

Standing on the cracked driveway, Simone knew she did not want to find a landline. She wanted to run in the other direction, keep going until she caught one solitary bar on her phone. Or knock awake one of the sleeping residents in the suburbs down below, get them to make the call. Anything to avoid going through the heavy front door.

Robin would not leave Montagu Breakspear though. He wouldn't pay attention to her superstitions. There'd be no turning him around now even if she grabbed the hair above each of his ears and tried to evoke older sister privileges.

However, the way she saw it, the old man wasn't going to die. He was already recovering from his wound. It had been half an hour at least and, instead of dying in their arms, he showed hopeful signs of life: his eyes were open and his lips trembled. He was going to be okay. They'd got him to where his butler said he'd be safe and they didn't have to do any more. She repeated it as a mantra around and around her mind.

Robin was on a mission. He would do all he could for this man. She understood; admired him for it. Nevertheless it raised dread within her.

Unmoving she let her eyes travel the full length of the heavy oak door. There was an inevitability she would walk through it.

"Excuse me, Miss Simone."

An apparition, as if from the air, Murkiss appeared beside Robin.

"Mr Robin, if you could please help me carry Mr Breakspear in, I should be most grateful." He was humble, an older gentleman seeking a young man's help and muscle.

"We will call an ambulance, right?" snapped Robin.

"Of course, sir."

"You said you would go to the hospital."

"I think this is the best place for him, sir. And you heard what he said on the pavement. Mr Breakspear has a long standing phobia of hospitals."

"He had his stomach slit open!"

"I know, sir. But I don't think the wound was as deep as you may have initially surmised. We are here already, and you can appreciate it would be better for Mr Breakspear to be inside in the warm, rather than out here in the cold and dark."

Robin was going to say something else, make another argument for nurses and doctors no doubt. She could have helped him, if she hadn't felt all words swallowed within her. Murkiss pre-empted both of them though, touching Robin solicitously on the arm.

"Trust me," the man's voice was little more than a murmur. "You are kind and I appreciate your concern towards Mr Breakspear. He will appreciate it too when he recovers. But I have been with him a long time and I know this house is the best place for him to recuperate. It is where he would most wish to be. Trust me," he repeated. "We can call the healthcare professionals if you want, but in a few hours he will be a new man."

It was the certainty of the voice which did it, or something in the man's eyes she couldn't see when they met Robin's. Her brother nodded once and then gathered Breakspear's body in his arms and carried him across the battered old driveway. Following in the butler's footsteps.

There was one step to the giant door and Breakspear grunted as Robin ascended it. A jarring of the wound perhaps, although Simone thought fancifully it might also be utter fear.

Her own irrational foreboding transferring onto the man who actually owned this house.

Murkiss pushed and the door opened. (Had they left it unlocked?) Then he walked into darkness, her brother behind him. Simone remained a few paces distant. The idea occurred that the enormous door might slam in her face before she reached it and, she inwardly confessed, she would be delighted if it did.

But no, she could step through into the cold, dank darkness of the epic hallway.

Then the door shut. The hinges creaking behind her and the catch of the lock echoing.

She did her best not to jump.

Only pale moonlight through the high-up crescent window illumined the hall. It didn't penetrate any of the shadowy corners and niches. The walls and the long wide staircase to the left of the front door adopted an ethereal glow.

Once inside, Murkiss's sturdy form found new and unexpected reserves of strength. He'd needed Robin to carry his master inwards, but once over the threshold he easily took him from Robin's arms. Again like he was felt and balsa.

The sound of their footsteps was absorbed by a thick, possibly red, carpet.

"Thank you, Mr Robin," he said. "I will make sure he is looked after. You can visit him shortly. However, if you want to put your mind at ease with a medical opinion, then be my guest. You will find a telephone through the second doorway on the right."

Then the butler strode from them up the staircase.

With concern on his brow, Robin watched Murkiss

and Breakspear ascend, and then he breathed in deeply.

When they heard a bedroom door above open and shut, he let out his breath and gazed around the grand, ostentatious hallway. She found herself exhaling too, glad to be rid of the creepy butler.

They heard a buzz before the bulbs of the chandelier burst into startling life. Murkiss must have hit the switch.

Her brother took a step backwards to take it all in.

"What do you think?" he asked.

CHAPTER SEVENTEEN

Simone both whispered and stuttered. "I think we shouldn't be here."

"I know. We get to the phone, get help and then…" He said the words, they crossed his lips, but his eyes were lost taking in the hallway's grandeur. Running an appraiser's eye across the wood panelling, the golden candle sticks and the grand old portraits hanging on the walls. "Although you heard what Breakspear said, he was clear on *no hospitals*."

"Was he?" she asked, her stomach roiling in knots. "Or was he saying two separate things? No to this place and then asking for a hospital?"

Robin hesitated. Confusion crossed his forehead, before he raised an eyebrow and let go a whistle. "We are where we are, darling."

"Don't call me darling!" she snapped. "This isn't a playful moment."

"Okay," He nodded in apology. "Maybe the butler is right. I wouldn't have imagined this when we got into the car, but it seems Breakspear could make a recovery.

Incredible given how old he is. Think of the reward he might offer us. He may very well want to fund The Fallowford Trust for the rest of his days."

Anger surged in her breast and she felt her cheeks flush hotly. She grabbed his arm and spun him around with all the force of a pissed off big sister. "What the fuck is wrong with you?"

"What do you mean?"

"You literally have the man's blood smeared on your hands. He nearly died on the pavement right in front of us. I was terrified he would die in the car. You were too! If you hadn't had your hands full looking after him, you'd have throttled that Murkiss character for ignoring what you were saying. How can you stand there now and be calm? How can you wander around here like – I don't know – you've come in from a game of tennis and have nothing more on your mind than Pimm's and fucking lemonade?"

He held up his hands. "I don't know what happened there. But I know what I saw when we got out of the car. I may have saved a life tonight, Si. *We* might have saved a life. Doesn't it make you feel good?"

"It's elation then? Maybe a mite premature, isn't it? You can't be certain he will live."

"I'm optimistic."

"And Murkiss ignoring your calls to go to the hospital? That man had his belly torn open by a kitchen knife. He's elderly and he needs proper medical treatment."

With an apologetic smile Robin tugged his arm from her grip. It didn't really need much exertion. He took a step forward and swung his eyes around again. "I know what you're saying, darling, but I heard him say 'no hospital'. Maybe it was different, but that's the way I heard it. And the butler said Breakspear would recover in this house and – you saw it – he was recovering in the car, so maybe he's right. And let's be honest, this Murkiss is his butler. He would hardly bring him here and let him die with witnesses in tow, would he?"

What the hell is wrong with you? She wanted to ask.

But she could see on his face at least part of the answer. It was this house, it bowled him over. No, it was more than that. Robin had always been a great admirer of wealth. It was both a drive and a flaw in him. Yet in normal circumstance, he would not have forgotten an incident like this so quickly he'd be examining furnishings within the hour. He was not that callous; not that solipsistic. Tonight there was something about this house which was speaking to him. It was affecting him in a way it wasn't her.

She could recognise the grandeur of the place of course. A space this big and well looked after must have plenty of cash behind it. The chandelier made everything gleam, from the panelling on the walls, to the glint at the edge of the paintings, to the gold entwined right through the bannister. There were little tables and display cases against all the walls. Each of them containing something which shone with the power of a Swiss bank account. 'Ostentatious' was the descriptor which sprang to mind. She imagined if she stopped to examine them, she'd find a Fabergé Egg or a Ming Vase. However, she remained unimpressed. To her it all seemed artifice. A show put on. Her immediate suspicion was this house had one pleasant room and it was the hallway, as that was the one which would impress the visitors. But, judging by the building's exterior, she suspected neglect. Perhaps beyond the big shiny hall would be room after room of shabby emptiness. Maybe one would have a stained mattress; another would have nothing more than an empty coke bottle. It didn't seem real to her. It was fool's gold and she hated to admit it, but apparently Robin was a bloody fool.

"I told you he had money, didn't I?"

"What?" she asked.

"Those claims he was on the edge of the poorhouse were exaggerated."

She stared at him.

"Don't you like it?" he asked.

"It's not really my taste," she sneered. "I think we need to get out of here. Let's go outside and I'll try to get reception on my mobile."

Without thinking she had stepped towards the front door – the carpet feeling unfeasibly warm under the soles of her shoes – but he was wandering his way further in. Making circles with his feet as he consumed all the space; taking in every item and, with an eye which would make many an auctioneer blush, working out how much they would cost. Her brother's mind was too easy to read. When you're from a family which used to have something but didn't anymore, you become good at determining how much others have. She was cursed with it too, although to a lesser extent. In Robin, she'd always admired the way he could do it without seeming a rat. Even those old ladies he took to bed knew he had evaluated them in every single way, but they still adored him for it.

Now she felt furious with him for the trait.

"I'll find a phone here," he said to pacify her, with no urgency at all. "But I don't want to leave this place until we know he's okay. Don't you want to know the man stabbed in front of you is on the path to recovery? Besides, given what happened – as well as what we've learned about the genuine state of his wealth – we might have to raise the subject of the reward ourselves."

His eyes circled again. Reflecting the shine of every valuable item. Cartoon pound signs practically rolling their way higher and higher in his gaze.

"Do you think he was expecting anyone?" he mused, as he ran his finger along a small table against the staircase which was loaded with various twinkling ornaments. There was no dust. "I mean look at this place. It seems like he's waiting for a party."

"Okay, I'm going," she said. "I'll walk down the driveway and get the bars on my phone and call an ambulance. Then a taxi. In that swift order. If Breakspear wants to send me a thank you note in the morning, he's more than welcome. But beyond that, Robin, this isn't worth anything more."

When he turned to her it was with a grin. "Darling, don't desert me. Let's linger longer. I'm sure Murkiss will be here in a minute with an update."

She sighed. Knowing she couldn't change his mind.

"Another thing," she said. "How did the butler know our names?"

"What?"

"He called me Simone and you Robin. We didn't introduce ourselves."

"When he was driving, he would have heard us talking to each other."

"I never call you Robin unless I'm pissed off. And when do you ever use my full name?"

His mouth opened and shut. He was trying to find an explanation or an excuse, but he had nothing.

"Please!" she said.

His hands went up to pacify her again, infuriating her all the more. "Okay, let me find the phone. Second door on the right, was it?"

He took three steps forward and leant on the high shined gold handle of a large white door. Then he stepped into the room beyond.

Alone in the hallway, she felt the silence sink down upon her

"Robin?" she called. "Rob?"

No reply.

She didn't wait more than five seconds. Against every instinct, she dashed across the hallway floor and followed him through the door.

Her heart lurched.

He wasn't there.

CHAPTER EIGHTEEN

Time had passed, Robin grasped this much, but he couldn't comprehend how much time or what had happened. A dizzy feeling swooped around and around his head. Dehydrated and with his ears ringing, his hand flailed for the nearest wall. He had the nauseous, rubber-legged feeling which follows a demon rollercoaster. The sense of speed and his stomach dangling somewhere in the clouds. He lurched forward, no longer trusting solid ground.

Having squeezed his eyes shut and tried to centre himself, the first thing he noticed when he opened them again was, to his right, a big, clean, bay window with sunlight streaming in through the panes. Actual daylight. Surely he'd been in the hallway with Si only seconds ago. But that had been the middle of the night. How could it now be morning? What had he been doing and why did the inside of his head appear to be his enemy rather than his friend?

The second thing he noticed was a strangulated screech. One of surprise and shock and sheer embarrassment. His gaze fell upon a naked woman.

She was perched on the edge of a king sized bed. Her arms wrapped tight around herself, her legs crossed.

Across this sparse room – which had little else of note beyond the window, the bed and the brilliant white walls – the two of them held each other's gaze.

Robin was being ungallant, he understood that, but he couldn't stop himself from staring. He knew he'd never seen her before, but she reminded him of a person he used to know. They were two different women, but it was there in the plumpness of her figure and the heart shape of her face. Even the way her blonde hair curled onto her shoulders. A lady he'd known intimately and retained fond memories of.

She was the first woman he'd been with after the accident. The aunt of a friend of his and so an older woman. A person who had shown him kindness when everyone else wanted to judge. There were long, angry nights when he hated himself and only made it through because he knew that Simone and this lady – Tina, her name had been – cared for him.

Their dalliance hadn't lasted. Relationships formed as much through trauma as sexual attraction rarely do, but she claimed a piece of his heart.

This woman wasn't Tina. For a start she was more the age Tina had been back then, rather than what she would be now. But the biggest difference was that he was sure if Tina saw him again, her face would be loaded with emotion. A remembered joy and a harboured regret mixed together. But this lady, her expression was surprised, but also had more than a touch of flirtation about it.

"Excuse me," he stammered. "I'm sorry."

His voice was shaky and he nearly called her Tina. That would have been a mistake. Or he thought so, until a voice at the back of his mind told him this woman was called Tina too.

How could that be? And how could he possibly know?

He pulled his hand from the wall and tried to stand upright, be the young vigorous man he was and not a drunken idiot. In his mind the certainty came that this woman *was* called Tina and, whereas she wasn't his once upon a time love, she was someone he'd met. He realised he'd lost a period of time, that he was missing several hours. Between standing in the hallway with Si and now, other events had occurred. But for whatever reason he couldn't focus on them.

The woman – this other Tina – tightened her arms around herself on the bed and her cheeks remained flushed. But when she spoke her voice was calm. "It's okay, I guess," she said. "It is easy to get lost in this bloody maze of a house!"

Her skin was pale and smooth. She was in her mid-forties, he estimated. If you were being uncharitable you would say she was heavy-set, but he admired a woman with a round shoulder. No doubt she was plumper than she'd been as a twenty-something, but she was shapely. Even with her chest covered by her arms, he could see it retained a pleasing pertness.

Once again his head spun dizzyingly and he found his palm pressing against the wall for support. "I'm sorry." He squinted at the daylight through the window. It was quite, quite dazzling. So much so, he couldn't make out anything beyond the glass. "I'm confused. I was just with my sister…"

"Simone?" she interrupted. "I heard she was going

to have a nap after breakfast?"

"Breakfast?" he asked. Then: "You've seen her?"

"Yes, she was exhausted after your exertions last night. I'm sure you both are."

"Exertions?"

"Well, what happened with Breakspear when he was stabbed. How you saved his life, brought him here and then came and joined us."

There were so many elements spinning around, that he could barely grasp hold of any of them. "You saw my sister at breakfast?"

"Yes, we had grapefruit and discussed broken hearts." She smiled, big. It lit up her entire face. "Simone seemed fine this morning. Tired, but relieved. She's stunning, isn't she?" she said, though her tone implied she was not sure if it was at all appropriate to compliment him on his sister's looks. "Anyway, I think I asked her about men and she corrected me on that score. Despite me being straight and her not, broken hearts are a universal language and we could talk in that. She looked around to see where you were, but given the amount you drank last night, neither of us thought you'd be one of the early birds."

"I drank last night?"

Her eyebrow raised, mocking but sympathetic too. She had wide dark chocolate coloured eyes. The other Tina had possessed those too. "You *do* have a hangover, don't you? It's not surprising. Cecil and Walter had to carry you to bed."

"Cecil and Walter?"

"Rugby players. You had a bit of a drinking game with them last night."

Did it mean he'd slept in a different room to Si? If he was as drunk as Tina said, then it wasn't a vast surprise. But it was amazing Simone let it happen. She would normally make sure she was there in case he woke. Undoubtedly she was shocked and drunk too, that was the explanation.

"How is Breakspear?" he asked.

"Oh, from what I hear he's fine." She spoke casually, pretending he'd suffered no more than a papercut.

"Okay," he said. "I'm sorry, are you a friend of his? Or an acquaintance?"

"We're friends," she beamed. "It takes a while for him to trust anyone. As I'm sure you've noticed. But once he does, he's a wonderful chum. When you arrived, several of us were having drinks in the lounge room. You came in, a right sight you were, covered in blood. We got you new clothes and then you and Simone joined us. We toasted the fact you were there to save Montagu."

Pulling himself from the wall, he examined his clothes. The white shirt he wore was much the same as the one he'd worn last night, although unstained. The trousers though were beige slacks. He imagined he must appear a raffish young man from the 1920s. It made him smile. Wasn't it the look he'd always gone for? For the first time since daylight assaulted his eyes that morning, his headache eased a little.

"Do you really not remember anything, Robin?"

He blushed and shrugged. "I'm afraid not."

"Oh," she said. "I'm a bit embarrassed, as you and I talked for a long while."

"Did we?" Then he blinked and grinned, pretending it was all coming to him. He couldn't remember it, but he could well imagine the exchange. Not only flirting with this naked woman, but propositioning her on first meeting. "Your name is Tina, isn't it?"

On the bed she nodded and then her smile turned into a broad grin. The most pleasant kind of awkwardness settled between them.

Tina was the one who broke it. Standing and in a casual, but beautiful gesture, letting her hands fall away from her. Without self-consciousness, showing him her wonderful voluptuous body.

"I was about to have a shower." Her voice had a sudden huskiness. "Possibly you can help me wash those difficult to reach places."

The headache felt a long ago memory and there was no way he could keep the smirk from his face.

CHAPTER NINETEEN

Simone's life was not one which lent itself to commitment, Robin apart. A fact which Lizzie already suspected. Circumstance had entwined her and Robin's lives far closer than most siblings. Once upon a time she had had to drop everything to rush home and look after him, and she had never stopped. Staying with him as he dragged her down this strange life path. The nature of what they did meant she moved around frequently. And when they headed to an airport, it was generally with no return flight booked. She might leave a city and not visit it again for years. Possibly never. Despite that, however, there were two women with whom she'd maintained long-term relationships. A year each, anyway. The first named Cassandra and the second Mathilde. She remembered them often, and with great tenderness.

But there was a third woman whose presence lingered in her mind. A beautiful and unsettlingly mysterious woman with whom she'd had a one-night stand in a Lisbon hotel room. A looker and a half. An

English woman, but a true Mediterranean beauty. Dark hair, eyes like strange sins, the face of a doll and a figure to win beauty pageants. This woman's looks alone meant she'd always have been a fond memory to Simone, but there was something else to her too. A peculiar sense of danger. In bed she was both gentle and rudely assertive. Yet mostly what Simone remembered was the air of cruelty to this woman, which was indefinable and yet unmistakably part of her allure. When she pictured her lying on top of the sheets, her nakedness offset by a large ruby choker she refused to take off, Simone couldn't help but both smile and shudder. She didn't know if the memory was pleasurable, or if it troubled her more each time she recalled it.

In the bar where they'd met and had an incredibly (and instantly) flirtatious conversation over Rioja, the lady had told her her name was Emilia and she was the widow of a famous horror author. But when Simone googled him later, she'd discovered the man had died decades ago, and so it had to be a story. Why she would tell it, Simone didn't know. What was the point of claiming to be the former wife of a long dead pulp writer no one had ever heard of? It added to the oddness of the experience.

Now, when Simone followed Robin through the door, she didn't find him. Instead, she found the long ago Emilia, startled besides a king-sized bed. She was dressed only in a black bra and knee-length tight black skirt, and had just shaken her thick brown locks over her shoulders. There was surprise on her face that anyone should disturb her, but the surprise turned into a flush of pleasure as she recognised Simone.

"Why, hello!" Emilia said, her eyebrow raised. "You

and I have met before, haven't we?"

So shocked was Simone by her long ago passion's sudden appearance, she barely registered the fact it was daylight outside. Or the fact her outfit had changed to a polka-dot summer dress. Her own hair tied in a ponytail.

All she could do was gawp at this vision before her. Emilia was as gorgeous and as glamourous as she remembered. Even make-up free. But as alluring as she was, there was also an aspect immediately unsettling about her. The two women fixed each other across the bare space of the bedroom. Emilia's dark eyes practically devouring her, while leaving Simone feeling a chill.

"I'm sorry," Simone spoke finally. "What are you doing here?"

Emilia took a step forward and grinned. "I could ask you the same question. I was changing in private when you burst in. Not that I necessarily mind, however."

"No!" Simone shook her head and tried to focus. Her mind was spinning, but she had to keep herself together. "This isn't right."

"What isn't?"

Simone hadn't ventured any further than the doorway, clinging on to the open door. To keep herself an escape option. To stop herself fainting with a thud to the carpet.

"I was following my brother," she spluttered. "I was right behind him. If he had come through this door and seen you, he'd be here, believe me."

Hands on hips, Emilia simpered, flattered. "Robin? Oh yes, he's a good-looking boy, isn't he? I think he's already made a friend."

"A friend?"

"Yes, you know the kind of friend he likes." The lascivious tone meant she didn't have to continue.

The two women regarded each other. Images from their long ago night flashed through Simone's mind. The way Emilia's feline cheeks rose suggested she knew exactly what Simone was thinking.

There was an incredible light flooding through the window, bright and harsh. An unnatural glare which Simone couldn't turn her head to regard. It made the ruby which Emilia once again wore tight around her throat gleam.

"Listen," Emilia said finally, "you had a tense night. A tough night. I truly can't imagine what you went through. But you're here and it's done. That old fart Breakspear will be fine. Why don't you relax a bit? Take your mind off all that's happened? I can help. I'm good at distractions."

She strode towards Simone, one long leg placed deliberately in front of the other, moving in the approximation of a catwalk model, hips sashaying.

"No!" Simone yelled and put her hand up to halt.

Emilia stopped, amusement on her wide lips. "No, what?"

"No, this!" snarled Simone. "No any of this!" She turned her head and peered into the brightness. Squinting at the intensity and not believing it for a second.

Part of the reason the memory of Emilia had lingered with her was there was melodrama wrapped around the woman. Just being with her briefly, you sensed you were entering someone else's grand, terrifying and unfathomable story. That even if you only had a bit part role, you had a good chance of being burnt. It's what made their fleeting encounter so memorable, and also what guaranteed Simone resisting Emilia's overtures to return the following night.

Emilia placed her hands on her hips. Chin raised high, showing off her features at their most defiant and magnificently attractive.

In contrast, Simone sank a little further into the doorway. Yet, oddly, she felt she was the one who had the power.

"What if I were to tell you," Emilia casually drawled her words, "that you and your brother arrived late last night with poor Breakspear in tow. You were shaky, unsure if you'd made the right move by not going to hospital. But then relieved when it transpired the old man would be fine. A few of us were already having drinks in the drawing room and you joined us there. Grateful for the alcohol and companionship after such a trying evening. Everybody drank too much. But the two of us stayed on opposite sides of the room. Of course we recognised each other, but we didn't reacquaint. Even with alcohol lowering our inhibitions. Indeed, this is the first time we've had a chance to speak, to recall the wondrous night we had together. Do you remember it? Lying there in the morning looking out across Lisbon. I'd have possessed you forever then if I could."

More cautious this time, she took another long pace forward. Close enough they could touch.

If Simone had wanted to, she could have reached out and taken Emilia in her arms. She'd have come more than willingly. Simone could have swooped on those plump lips, run her fingers through her thick lustrous hair, pulled her close and made quick work of getting her skirt and bra off. Actually, the way Emilia was returning her gaze, she saw it would be a race to see who could get the other naked first. One which Emilia was intent on winning. All Simone had to do was open herself up and then the morning could be spent rolling around the bed with one of the most beautiful creatures she had ever seen in her life.

Instead, her flat palm rose and she screamed at the top of her voice. "No!"

Emilia dropped her weight a little onto her left hip, a resigned move. The knowingness did not however disappear from her face.

When she spoke, her voice sounded distant, not really hers. "I haven't fooled you at all, have I?"

It needed a deep breath for Simone to catch herself, to answer in the approximation of a civil tone. "None of this is real, is it?"

"The house is real," said the creature pretending to be Emilia. "As for me, I'm as real and compliant as you want me to be." Her lips blew a kiss.

"No!" Simone jumped in revulsion. "Where's Robin?"

"Oh, what he has is real. For him, anyway. He has met a friend. She's entertaining him right now, and he's having the time of his life."

"Where is he?"

Emilia turned from her with a shrug, all her sex appeal vanishing. As alluring as a badly moulded piece of clay. "Oh, he's around. You better try and find him, hadn't you?"

A final glance passed between the women. One final come hither look from the temptress in the black bra, answered by a steeliness from Simone.

She retreated into the hallway and slammed the door behind her.

CHAPTER TWENTY

Back in the hallway, darkness subsumed her. All light fell away, and it left her in complete blackness. The chandelier had extinguished. Through the crescent window, the moonlight too appeared to have been switched off.

Disorientated, she felt her entire insides being tumbled around. Her legs were so weak she feared her bones might break and her muscles pop.

Frantically she threw out her arms and touched something solid. A wall - big, heavy and reassuring. Then she took a series of rasping deep breaths, not caring if the surrounding air tasted old and stale. Gradually she perceived shapes in the darkness. The base of the bannister and maybe, if she squinted, the front door ahead. She felt how chilly her bare arms were and the sticky dampness of her dress. Breakspear's blood! It meant she was back in her clothes. There was an odd reassurance in her hair being wild.

What the hell was this place? She quelled the urge

to scream as she knew, if she did, she'd block her own thoughts. All she'd achieve if she opened her lungs would be a surrender into panic. She needed to focus.

First thing she had to do was find Robin. Then, swiftly afterwards, get them both the hell away from this madhouse.

What was the room she'd just been into? How had it been daylight? How could *that* woman, of all women, be there? Most importantly of all, what had happened to Robin?

She squinted, but there were only a few vague shapes in the distance to guide her. A couple of minutes ago the room had been littered with occasional tables, display cases and the kinds of items you see people cooing admiringly at on antique shows. She didn't want to step forward and topple face first onto a sharp corner. But nor could she simply stand where she was.

Slowly, reaching to the side with one hand while the other stretched in front of her, she took a step forward. There was a creak underneath, and she realised she was walking on bare floorboards. Surely earlier there had been a thick red carpet, although – impossibly – it seemed to have been stripped back.

Only details, however. What it *appeared* to be was utterly irrelevant. She had to keep her tasks front of mind and not get distracted by anything else. Find Robin, get the hell out of there. She didn't add it as an extra task on her list, but 'not come back' was definitely third on her agenda.

Simone took another quick step forward, her fingers trailing on the wall until she felt – with a gasp – part of the brickwork crumble.

It flaked under the lightest of brushes. She had been

only dimly aware that she wasn't touching the wood panelling they'd seen on entering. Instead, it was rough and coarse brick, both cold and old. The elements having worked unceasingly against it over time. Part of it crumbled and hit the floor with a rat-tat-tat of pebbles. Then the surrounding house groaned, a deep sigh which seemed to contract the big black space around her. Making everything smaller. Trapping her.

Suppressing panic, she grabbed her fingers from the wall. For a second it felt like the brickwork had pulsed beneath her fingertips. That the damage she'd inadvertently caused wasn't just to masonry, it was a physical wound and there was red, angry flesh underneath.

Simone took a hurried couple of steps forward and thankfully didn't topple over some vintage hall stand and smash her face to the floor. She clenched her hands to her sides, trying not to brush against anything else. It meant her other senses were keener and therefore open when the smell came. The stench rose from beneath her feet and sank down from the darkness above simultaneously. An intense fetid odour of rotting and decay. Carrion abandoned for weeks until it was so rancid even desperate vultures would not nibble at it.

It was impossible not to breathe it in. Nor for the putrefying taste to flood her mouth, making her gag. She bent double at the waist, vomiting over her shoes. After the first heave she had to take another deep gasp of putrid air, and then she kept puking until there was only bile passing her lips.

She stumbled to her side and collapsed to the wall. Then she shrieked when, with an orgasmic groan, the brick yielded to her. Not as soft and warm as she could have received from Emilia, but an embrace nonetheless.

Above her came the noise of a pleasurable sigh mixed in with mocking laughter.

Limbs like jelly, she threw herself into the centre of the black hallway and only just held her balance. What stopped her crumpling to the floor was the dread it too might reach up and hold her. That it might take pleasure from the warmth of her body. Her hand clamped over her own lips until her screams were muffled.

Tears streaming from her eyes, she blinked and saw a glimmer of moonlight ahead of her. Penetrating the darkness at last. It was faint through the crescent window above the door, but it was something she could follow. A path to salvation. She could go outside, run the length of the driveway until her mobile worked and then call for help. Then, in the morning, she could find Robin. This place must look different in daylight. Proper, real daylight. Everything would be better and safer in the morning.

But no. Simone took two hurried paces forward and then brought herself to a halt. She knew with utter clarity that she couldn't leave Robin in here for so much as three hours. Even in the daylight, this place wouldn't feel safe. She had to find Robin first. It was the two of them together, just as it had been when they were kids, just as it had been since the accident. She wasn't walking through the door without him.

Not thinking of the sick on her shoes or the tearstains on her cheeks, she spun around. The darkness in the room was impenetrable, a sheer oppressive gloom. There was no illumination from moonlight in that direction. Trying to calculate the distance and the steps she'd need, she did her best to determine how to make her way back to the troublesome doorway.

What would happen if she walked through it again? Surely it wouldn't be Emilia once more. She didn't think so, but nor did she really believe Robin would be there either. Maybe it would be another woman to tempt her. A version of Lizzie, perhaps, offering safer – and more difficult to resist – pleasures.

If she rejected whatever or whoever awaited her, what would be next? Would the house eventually get bored enough it would take her to Robin? She had to know. She had to try.

Tentatively, she took a few steps forward and nearly lost herself to screaming.

In the darkness, both looming from it and standing impassive, was the broad, squat form of Murkiss.

His round, moon-shaped face utterly blank. When he spoke, his voice was emotionless.

"Can I help you, Miss Simone?"

CHAPTER TWENTY-ONE

Not far in a geographic sense, but miles distant in any practical reality, Robin was dreaming.

It was the sweetest of dreams. He was wrapped in the arms of a beautiful older lady; her round bosom crushed warm to his chest, while the caresses of her hands rendering him wonderfully safe. There was only the two of them in the world. No distractions, his mind not spinning off elsewhere. He was not with her under any ulterior motive. There wasn't part of his mind pondering on this woman's bank account. Instead, there was only enjoyment and pleasure – it was life the way in fantasies he lived it.

He buried himself into this image. Reassured himself how blissful it was. Tried to ignore the niggling worry forcing its way into his subconscious.

He had been to many cities, met numerous interesting people (more disreputable than reputable, but always interesting) and slept with more women than he could count without taking an hour to consider it. But a dream of such carnal pleasure was rare.

Normally his happiest dreams concerned childhood. His beautiful mother, always smiling, proud of him no matter what. In these night-time imaginations, his father was a friendlier person. No worries pushing down his shoulders, and with a far keener understanding of how to have a conversation with his son. Then there was Simone – or Si, as she'd always been then. Once upon a time she had turned her nose up at her full name and, to be fair, it had hardly suited her. She was a tomboy until the age of thirteen. Climbing trees, playing football and ready to clout anyone who she considered wasn't giving her enough respect. (One of Robin's arms was forever bruised from punches.) For her, every day was an adventure. There was always more trouble for her to get into. And she had never minded him tagging along. It gave her a cohort. As for him, he knew he couldn't be happier with a real brother than he was with the fearless Si.

These were the sunny places he normally retreated to.

But the way this woman's arms and legs enveloped him, as if she had more than the four limbs, was incredible too.

Most of the time he didn't have sweet dreams – not carnal, nor wonderful memories of sun-dappled childhood.

He was cursed with nightmares.

And they were always the same.

Reliving the accident.

There he was sat in that ditch. Dazed, shocked, blood flowing from the wound just inside his scalp, where he'd smacked his face into the steering wheel. Unable to move, he watched the other car. The one he'd hit at speed.

The smell of petrol was rich in the air, as was the aroma of blood and fear.

Trapped in the mangled wreckage, he waited for the other car to explode, knowing he could do nothing to alter it. Hours seemed to pass where he sat and stared at it and knew what would come, but had no way to stop it. In real life it had been a matter of seconds. But in every one of his nightmares, the torture was endless. There were two people sat before him who were going to burn to death. No matter what he did, he couldn't save them. He had to watch their skins fry and their innards boil.

Each night he tried to think of something he could do to save them.

But it was utterly hopeless.

In most of those nightmares, the couple in the other car screamed. They could smell the petrol too, see the sparks of fire and anticipate what was coming for them. There were hours of agony where, trapped and petrified, they yelled franticly at the top of their lungs. Calling for Robin to do something to save them. He was the one who'd hit them, it was his fault they were in that predicament. They were going to die because of him, and the very least he could fucking do was try to save them. But it was impossible. He couldn't move. When the engine blew, the entire car caught alight and then charred them like an oven.

However, there were other nightmares – far worse – where they didn't scream. Not only did they not yell or panic, they sat motionless and let the flames consume them. Both of them immobile, only their eyes showing any sign of life. Eyes fixed, unyielding on Robin,

Judging him, cursing him, silently wishing him nothing but pain and suffering for the rest of his miserable life. Hoping he met as atrocious an end as the one he'd so thoughtlessly foisted upon them.

Those were the worst nights. To not only relive those terrible images, to watch them die repeatedly, but to feel their utter hatred as they succumbed.

Although the bed was warm and the embrace deliciously soft, Robin shot out of his sleep with a cry. Shaking from a nightmare which was constant and unendurable.

Hands were on his torso in an instant. Calming fingers. For a few dazed seconds he thought a couple of ladies were trying to sooth him back towards the pillow, more than one set of hands. But it must have been a trick of his barely awake mind.

"Ssshhh," said Tina's voice, seeming to come from all around him. "You need not have a bad night's sleep. Not here."

He shook his head. "Si," he mumbled.

"See what?"

He gave no reply, merely let the hands lull him onto the bed.

But sleep would not come. He knew that.

CHAPTER TWENTY-TWO

Simone backed away. She didn't tumble off her heels. She didn't think so anyway. It was strange; she thought she was standing, but it seemed to be that Murkiss – the short, squat, little man – was towering above her.

In most ways he appeared the same: the bald head, the round face, the posture of bowed deference. But now she had to peer up at him. To crane her neck. He was a giant to her, so much so it seemed impossible for him to fit into the grand hallway. But at the same time, he was occupying the same space he'd always done.

It was more than size, she realised, it was a presence. This wasn't a man in front of her. He may have played the part of a humble servant, yet he was much more.

"Miss Simone?" he asked. "Is there anything I can help you with?"

She nearly turned and scrambled toward the front door. Gratifying the temptation to flee. All it would require was a dozen paces, and she'd be outside. She could run in the main road's direction, waving her arms and screaming at the top of her voice. A lunatic raving.

Sometimes it was good to give in to panic.

But no, she hadn't run before and she would not run now.

"My brother!" she said, not keeping the fear from her tremulous voice. "I want to see my brother."

"Mr Robin? I'm afraid Mr Robin is" – the look which crossed his face was loaded with meaning – "otherwise engaged."

His tone, a kind of dismissive familiarity – followed by a chuckle to himself – grated. Rising amidst her fear was irritation. It helped hold her feet steady. Gave her voice an affronted curtness.

"I want to see him!"

"I'm afraid it is utterly impossible at this juncture, Miss Simone."

"What does that mean?"

He blushed and shook his head bashfully. "I doubt he would appreciate an appearance from either you or I at this point. I think it's better to allow him a spot of privacy. He would appreciate it, I'm sure."

But her gaze held firm, her expression hardened. Behind her, she was vaguely conscious of the moonlight streaming through the crescent window becoming brighter. It became an almost ethereal glow. The light at the end of the tunnel she should escape to. Outside appeared to be nothing but clear, beautiful sky. A breath-taking night. One to dance around in and enjoy, rather than argue with intransigent butlers.

Still however, she held firm.

"He'll want to see *me*!"

Murkiss demurred and coughed politely. "If I might be bold enough as to suggest, Miss Simone, that your attentions may be better channelled elsewhere. Your young teacher friend is lonely tonight. My understanding is she believed she would sleep easily, but is instead lying alone and awake in her comfortable bed. Pining for you. A call at this point would be gratefully appreciated. Then you and your brother can reconvene in the morning, both feeling – ahem – refreshed."

Her face must have twisted in revulsion. How could he could know that? How was it possible for him to be aware of Lizzie? She felt sick and violated. This was her life, and he was tossing it around as if it was a cheap bauble.

Simone could have screamed at him then, but through painful effort, she kept her voice small and tight. Speaking slowly, she repeated herself. "He'll want to see me!"

"Have you considered, Miss?" he asked conversationally, "that it might be time for a touch of independence. For both you and Mr Robin. Far be it for me to presume, but having seen close siblings in the past, I know there comes a time when even the strongest bond needs to be cut. It will never be truly severed, yet it will be beneficial for both parties if you seek your own paths in the world."

Her shoulders shook and the fury burnt in her eyes. "What the fuck can you know of my relationship with my brother?"

"I've learned a great deal since you entered my house."

"*Your* house?"

"Mr Breakspear's house," he corrected himself with swift, but false, modesty.

"Where's Robin?" she yelled.

"I know it must be a tad frustrating, Miss Simone, but really there is no need for hysterics. Patience is a virtue and he will contact you in due course."

She was at her full height, shoulders thrust back. Murkiss still towered above her, but he must have seen there was no surrender in her.

"You really want me to leave this house, don't you?"

"Given the circumstances, I think it might be for the best, yes. I know I am a representative of the host and this may seem unforgivably rude, but come morning I feel sure all parties will appreciate it was the correct choice."

"Where is the host?" she demanded. "Where is Breakspear? Can I at least see him?"

He considered for a few seconds, and then those plump lips of his pursed into a smile. "Do you know, Miss Simone?" he said. "I think that could be a wonderful idea. I'm sure Mr Breakspear can explain to you, in a way I seem incapable of, how things work around here."

CHAPTER TWENTY-THREE

Such was the awfulness of most of Montagu Breakspear's life, he had long quit determining where his nightmares ended and his real painful existence began. To him, they were one and the same.

Once again he sat at the edge of his bed, wearing nothing but his underpants and staring at his wounds. This time there was a gash across his stomach, his navel had been unzipped both ways across his belly. He prodded at it nervously with his forefinger. It felt different from most of the other injuries. This one would not be forgotten easily, nor mixed in with the other scars. No, he would feel this every time he moved, every time he breathed. The house would not let him forget that as long as he was living, there would be fresh suffering awaiting him.

When he closed his eyes and tried to recall what had happened, he was surprised by the realisation that the wound was inflicted beyond the realm of the house. There had been an angry, bald man spinning startled on his heel with a blade in hand.

Who the hell was he?

All his years in the house, all the different faces which had taken turns torturing him, and yet he had never seen this one. Also, the house had never chosen to hurt him outside the walls before. (Although he knew, of course, that if he stayed away too long, it would suck him dry.) This then was something new. It shook him. He thought he'd lost the capacity to feel surprise, but this – whatever it was – was hardly a pleasant development.

With the bald man, being harassed by him in fact, was a woman. Breakspear squinted uncomfortably at the recollection. She was real; he was sure of it. A striking, raven haired beauty. One he'd given the shortest of shrifts to in recent times. What was she doing in his dreams? What would she be doing in his reality? Yet in the flashes of his mind, there she was. Swooping in on him and crying for help.

Finally, there was a young man. Her brother, he realised grimly. Only now, rather than the naked hunger the young man had displayed on their first meeting, there was concern and compassion. He had placed his hands on Breakspear's guts, attempted to staunch the bleeding. Unaware that, until this house had a better option, it would look after him.

What was he remembering? Everything which happened to him inside the house – every torture – felt excruciatingly real. They weren't though. That's how the house was so easily able to reassemble him. But this was different. He stroked his fingers across the healing wound once more and knew it had really happened to him. His blood had genuinely been shred on the comparative safety of the street.

The awfulness of most of Montagu Breakspear's life

meant he had done his best to stop feeling. This was why the tortures of the house had become more elaborate, to try to reach him. Now he felt something. A proper nagging pain, combined with a strange relief he'd made it to the house unharmed. That he could use this as an excuse to hide himself.

His smooth fingers ran across the wound, and then he flinched. Conscious he wasn't alone, expecting Murkiss to be glowering at him.

But no!

It wasn't Murkiss. Instead, it was the young, beautiful woman from the casino, standing in a blood stained green dress.

His blood.

He gave a yelp of sheer terror.

There was another human being within the walls of Breakspear Hall!

CHAPTER TWENTY-FOUR

At first glance, Simone didn't recognise him.

Not only had Breakspear already recovered from the slash deep into his abdomen, he had – in the space of a few hours – become forty years younger.

His hair was dark brown, almost to the point of black, and – even though he looked to have only just raised his head from the pillow – it was slicked back and immaculate. His skin was olive tanned and smooth, almost beautifully so, not a blemish apparent. His was a long face, but handsome. He had a heavy brow, an aquiline nose, full but oddly bloodless lips and a strong rounded chin. If one of those features had been more prominent, then it would have distorted his looks. As it was, all worked together perfectly. Even sitting down she could tell he had gained no height, but he was certainly broader – the muscles of his chest and arms more prominent. The hard body of an athlete. A man who could jump from that bed and have no qualms about doing one hundred press-ups.

The transformation was impossible. Robin had said

he was in his eighties and he'd looked every year of it. The idea flashed through her mind that this was a son they didn't realise the old man had, but she knew in the same instant it wasn't. On the bed in front of her was Montagu Breakspear.

His narrow gaze watched her with similar recognition. Undoubtedly he was handsome and, if she was another woman, she might have found him attractive. There was a darkness to him, beyond his saturnine looks, which probably would have been part of the appeal. But there was also, despite his smooth skin, a quality so incredibly old to him. His face showed its recognition, but it also washed full with regret and self-hatred. A lifetime's worth. Several lifetime's worth, she felt.

Suddenly he stretched his arm and grabbed her hand, clutching it tight between his fingers. Pulling her forward onto her toes, he brought her hand swiftly to his lips. She thought he would kiss it, slobber all over her. Maybe it was briefly his intention, but instead he held it to his face, squeezed his eyes shut and just about held away the tears.

"I'm sorry," he said. "I'm so sorry. My entire life I have tried to keep the front door locked. It got harder and harder. They sent me into the world. Looking, hunting, seeking someone new. But I resisted. I knew it would cost me when I came back here. I would suffer for it, but I didn't want anyone else through those doors. All my life I've done my best to stop it. However, now..." Tears didn't come, but his voice choked as he hunted for more composure. "Who was the man with the knife?" he asked suddenly. "He wasn't with you, was he? Who was that man?"

He let go of her hand at much the same time as she

wrenched it away. His voice as a young man was aural caramel, smooth and rich. She could imagine it broadcasting over the BBC.

Behind them, though he kept the pretence of the humble butler, she saw Murkiss was struggling to hide his amusement.

"Miss Simone to see you, sir."

Breakspear had asked her questions, but she had a big one of her own. "What the fuck is going on?" she demanded.

From the bed, he goggled at her, aghast. His generation clear in his reaction. Apparently he found it appalling that a young lady would ever swear. "That man he wasn't with you, was he?" he croaked.

She didn't answer.

His features twisted into an indescribable expression, caught between a grimace and a smile. "He wasn't, was he? But his actions sent you into my house. The thing there," Breakspear nodded disdainfully toward Murkiss, "must be delighted. Absolutely delighted."

The room was desperately sparse, she realised. It was like visiting a condemned man in his cell. The walls were grey and unadorned; the bed was the only item of furniture and it sat in the middle of the room on splintered and rotting floorboards. She did her best not to consider the smell, a bouquet of damp mixed with disgusting old sheets on a stained mattress. The notion she'd had on entering the house of everything beyond the opulent hallway turning out to be ruined and decayed was dispiritingly correct.

"Will you listen to me?" she said, trying to keep a level of patience. Knowing screaming and yelling would be cathartic, but wouldn't prise her from this mess. "*He*" – Breakspear shuddered on being forced to regard Murkiss – "told me you'd explain what is going on here."

He blinked at her, infuriatingly lost in his own thoughts. "You shouldn't be here. No matter what happened, you shouldn't be here." He shook his head frantically, wishing her from the room. "Why did you want to know me?" His mind found itself on a new track. "That's the question I asked you, wasn't it? Why did you want to know me?"

"It's not important! I need to find my brother. He's lost in here. You need to help me find him!"

The two of them stared at each other. Both lost in their own concerns.

Murkiss lingered only a few feet away, and she thought he wanted the anger to flare between them. For them to put brick walls against the other and slam their skulls repeatedly into them. Perhaps it was the butler's naked desire which calmed them both, brought them back from the edge. They could each sense it and neither wanted to give the satisfaction.

A kindness appeared for the first time in Breakspear's gaze. He focused on her, his youthful body stooped at the shoulders.

"I will help you," he spoke in a tremulous voice. "I will do what I can as it has been my life's work to stop exactly this happening. But please, before I do – because we need honesty between us – you have to answer my question. What was it you wanted from me?"

She didn't hesitate, embracing a bluntness she'd never used before. "We're con people," she confessed. "We wanted your money."

At first he didn't understand, the confusion was evident, but then the idea made its way through and he found it hysterical. The laughter contorted his features, aging him decades again and making him look quite mad. "You want my money? Only money? You can have it! You can take it all for the good it will do you in this place."

CHAPTER TWENTY-FIVE

Breakspear calmed himself slowly, running his hands through his fine head of hair and pulling his fingers back to check it wasn't all falling out. Then he raised his gaze to meet hers once more.

His eyes were all determination. He was willing strength into them,

"You want to know what is going on in this house?" his voice rumbled.

Simone nodded.

"Then I will have to give you a history lesson." He took a deep breath. "You are keen to find your brother, are you not?"

"Yes."

"If he's trapped alone in this house, then I am eager to locate him too. But you need to know what you are dealing with."

"Tell me!"

He shifted uncomfortably on those dirty sheets.

She leaned against the wall and crossed her arms, waiting.

Both of them tried to ignore the continued presence of Murkiss.

"Something unspeakable happened here in the 1920s." Breakspear was intoning, voicing words which had been in his mind for decades, but which he had never got close to uttering before. "I've never determined quite what. This building was a school and my grandfather was its proprietor and headmaster at the time. He did leave a journal, but to read it… Well, they are the ramblings of a madman. He talks of a ritual and of a boy dying. Not as an accident, but as an event he wanted. An outcome he craved. Then he writes of an ancient evil flooding from below and seizing possession of the house. I don't know what he was trying to achieve. At points his journal is impenetrable. It seems he believed there was something in this house. Outside man's comprehension. A passage to beyond the veil and it was his mission to open it.

"When he purchased the building, it was with that in mind. The architect was a notorious occultist. But my grandfather gave it our family name, so when he had success in his experiments, it would never be forgotten who the genius behind it was. And he opened a school, not to teach young boys of the Edwardian era how to become fine gentlemen, but so he'd have little sheep in a line whose blood he could use for his own purposes."

"Jesus!" she exclaimed softly.

"He was successful in his experiments, I think. Although his triumph left him broken. The story goes that when parents arrived one Friday afternoon seeking to take their child away for the weekend, they found said child was missing and my grandfather was naked in his study, gibbering while he ate his own faeces."

"That's disgusting," she breathed.

"I agree. His quest was dark and immoral, and destroyed his mind. But somewhere along the line, he achieved his aims and cursed my family forever."

He shook his head mournfully.

"The house passed to my uncle. The old head teacher's eldest son from a long ago marriage. A child, one of two, whom he had made no effort to support. This young man was his rightful heir. I never met him, but my father told me he was a hangover from the Victorian era. Starched shirts and everything in proper working order – or else. What had happened here must have offended both his faith in religion and the way things were simply supposed to be. But he made the best of it he could. For a while he kept the school open. A decision which, from a reportedly quite learned man, was irredeemably stupid.

"The child who was missing had actually been slaughtered in the study. With money and I imagine a certain amount of charm, my uncle covered it up. Bribed the nurse in the infirmary, informed the parents of the dead boy that he'd been taken by a sharp dose of influenza and he was sorry for their loss. Repaid their fees in full. He put about the story that his father's illness was an apoplexy from working too hard. But his attempt at salvage was wasted effort. This place couldn't continue as a normal school, no matter how honourable my uncle's intentions. There was a presence in this house now. A force which couldn't be put back. An eldritch power which made it in no way safe to have small boys around.

"He tried. For six months he tried, with pale and terrified children begging to move to another school in every letter to their parents. It was unsustainable, and eventually my proud uncle realised it. By then he knew something terrible had been unleashed. But equally he had the family's good name to consider. This was Breakspear Hall, after all. It held the name of our ancestors. A scandal would not be welcome. He dismissed the pupils, repaid everyone's fees, wrote references for the staff and gave them excellent severance payments so they wouldn't speak ill of the place. Then he shuttered the doors permanently.

"I never met the man himself, but I feel he was an honourable gentleman. He tried to do what was right. I don't know what he went through all those years by himself, but part of me can understand it."

"We had a family name too," she told him. "It can be tarnished. You recover."

"Who were your people?"

"I don't see how it's important," she blurted. But when she realised he wasn't going to go on without an answer, she conceded: "*My* great, great grandfather was an investor in The City at the turn of the century. He made a lot of money, was in the papers for having a glamorous American actress wife, and so also had a name. That's all gone now. My grandfather squandered it all. Both the money and the name. You can't let it taint you."

"Ah, but you're a world apart from my uncle. He'd have considered you nouveau riche. There were Breakspears at Agincourt, you see? We are mentioned in The Doomsday Book." He tried for a smile. "I would agree with you – now. Towards the end of his life, it seems likely my uncle would have agreed with you too. I don't know. He died alone in this house. You will not understand what he went through between these walls, but I have come to know the horror of it all too well.

"At death there was no will. Perhaps he believed that when he died, whatever was in this house would expire with him. But he had two nephews. The children of the mad old headmaster's younger son. My father, now deceased. There was an obvious line of succession. The eldest of those nephews, my brother, stepped through those doors downstairs to gain possession and from that point it doomed him."

"I heard about the murders," she said.

"From the first I saw it, I knew it was an ugly house." He paused, musing, his voice raspier. "I spent a good portion of my youth in Tuscany. Have you been?"

"I have, although I don't really want to talk about globe-trotting."

"That was long, long ago," he said. "Another world, another life, but I have always remained fascinated by Italian architecture. English gothic does nothing for me. Nothing at all. I have always considered this house an eyesore. However, it's nothing compared to what awaits you once inside. We'd had no contact with my uncle when we were growing up, and so my brother had zero preparation for what awaited him." He paused.

Simone waited. Trying to be patient.

"At first the house lures you in," he said finally. "You take possession of it and it rolls out all kinds of unimaginable pleasures. Between these walls I have enjoyed decades of carnality and eroticism."

The bald statement clearly took her aback, however she didn't blush. After a moment's pause he squinted at her expression closely, to see if he was okay to continue, whether she was mortally offended by what he'd said. But she simply nodded and said, unemotionally, "Go on."

"I don't know how much time I lost in such unnatural decadence. I look at the promising young man I once was and can scarcely credit I gave in so easily. But then men are weak, I suppose. By the time I realised what was happening to me, how far I had fallen, it was too late."

"Why?" she asked. "Why was it too late?"

"The reason being this house has drained me. Sucked all my promise and strength. It has taken everything from me. I may look in fine fettle. When I'm between these walls, I generally do. Outside, well, the illusion is harder to maintain. The house is still draining me, it still needs me – as its owner – to feed it. But it requires more energy from me over distance. I look more my age in the sunlight of the real world, but I don't appear anywhere near as old as I feel. I am ancient. When I move there is a deadness to me, my soul is rotted. I am much older and more broken than I could possibly appear, even outside.

"If I was away from this house for too long, it would drain me to a shrivelled husk, I know that. It needs me to be present, or not too far away for long. The notion has occurred that I could try to stay absent for weeks or months or maybe even years. Push my body to the edge. To the point where the powers within this house cannot stop a collapse. Where it could not possibly keep me alive. But how long would it take? When every inch of you aches with unspeakable fatigue, you do crawl to comfort. Even when the comfort is as horrible as mine."

He rubbed his fingers across his belly. "You were there when I sustained the knife wound last night, weren't you? I remember."

"I was." She said, then added, "It wasn't last night, it's still dark. It's the same night. A long, endless fucking night."

This time he restrained his reaction to her swearing.

"Did you think I would die?" Breakspear asked, meekly.

"I did."

He tightened his lips, scrunching his features sadly and apologetically. "It wouldn't let me die. It looks after its own. Once upon a time a burglar broke into this place. Came through the window. Why he concluded it would be a promising target, I do not understand, but he did. The house did not appreciate that. It didn't like the idea of me threatened, or it violated. Undoubtedly the latter more than the former. This felon arrived with a crowbar and a knife. The house made him swallow both and kept him alive while those sharp pieces of metal worked their way through his digestive tract. I heard his screams for days afterwards. I think it believed the man's agonies would fill me with pleasure."

He turned in the direction of the silent Murkiss.

The butler's round face dipped, as if to say: "You're welcome."

"But it's let us in here," she said. "It's taken Robin." Her lower lip trembled. "It's not going to torture him, is it?"

"No. I think it has hopes for you."

"What hopes?"

"An heir," he expunged the words from his lungs. "I am the last of the Breakspears. The first since my family took hold of this godforsaken house to have no heirs whatsoever. I have no brothers, nor nephews, nor cousins. Nor do I have friends. At first because I was so entranced by what was on offer here, I didn't need any friends. Later, when my mind righted myself, it was because I knew I could bring no one through these doors. But I am an old man. This house might be able to make me look young, it might be able to rejuvenate me after injury, but it simply *cannot* keep me alive forever. *That* is beyond even its power. It wants someone younger, a person who can take possession of it and it can take possession of. A new man to laughably call 'Master'."

She shuddered. "Oh, God… Robin."

With reluctance and sadness, Breakspear nodded. Then he continued his narrative:

"My brother kept this place for thirty years. We did not speak for nearly all of the period. I don't know when his mind snapped. But I think it was his plan to do something horrible and have the house taken from him. He would not leave it to me, he would lose it instead."

"Couldn't he have started a fire?" she asked.

He scoffed and looked at the bare, grubby window. Then, with a creaking of limbs which was utterly incongruous in such a young-looking man, he forced himself to his feet. His underwear hanging saggy towards his knees. Wincing, he made his way to the window, his muscles loosening as he walked. But not enough for him to convince as the young, athletic man he outwardly resembled. He peered through the glass, but she got the impression there wouldn't be much to see. Not simply because it was dirty and the night still dark, but for the fact the house didn't want him – or anyone – to dwell too much on the wider world.

"If there were curtains here, you *could* set fire to

them," he mused. "But you'd watch with wonder as no great flames took hold. No, you couldn't burn it, you couldn't light explosive within it, I doubt very much if you could hit it with a bulldozer in any meaningful way. No, you would need to do something dark and drastic. I cannot condone what my brother did, but I understand the point he had reached when he did it.

"He was deranged." He turned to her. "But when he killed those men, he was hoping the proper authorities would seize the house. That investigators would come in and take it off him to pay legal costs. Ideally, the entire property would be ripped from his hands and disposed of. But this wasn't the way the law worked. Regardless of what he'd done, it found its way to me."

"And you kept it for yourself?"

"I kept other people away!" he said, affronted. "I did what I had to. I kept people from here. When I got older and it made itself clear as to what it wanted, when *that creature,*" he snarled at Murkiss "uttered its demands, I refused. I did my utmost to never get close to anyone, to not give into the demands of this accursed house. Nobody came home with me. I succeeded. *Right until last night.*"

He tried to glare at her, but it came without force. His anger was plain to see, but she wasn't the actual target.

"And it wants Robin to take possession?" she asked.

"I believe so. Young blood. What it's been waiting for."

"But I'm the older sibling. Aren't I the logical candidate?"

Breakspear shook his head. "Forget logic, it won't help you here. This old house doesn't appreciate women. Misogynist, probably. Possibly because it used to be a boy's school. More likely because they're harder to control. Women are less in thrall to their desires."

"But, but, but... You and he are not related, how can you leave it to Robin?"

"You can leave a house to whomever you choose. What exists between these walls is ancient and primal. It will not need a solicitor's letter or precedent to make a legacy binding. If it decides I've passed on possession to your brother, then it would have its fondest wish. It would have a new owner. A new soul to torment and drain of life. Everything would have worked beautifully for it."

"Okay," she said, urgency in her tone. "Enough story time. We have to find him. We have to do *something.*"

He nodded. There was an old, thick dressing gown on the bedstead and he took three tottering steps towards it. "The house cannot hide him forever. We have to hope it cannot hide him long enough."

It was then the silence of Breakspear Hall was ripped apart by Robin's screams.

CHAPTER TWENTY-SIX

Slowly Robin had pried himself free.

The woman he was with, who was curled around him, was gorgeous. (Although it embarrassed him to realise he couldn't immediately recall her name again. Tina, was it?) The wide, contented smile she gave made clear she'd do anything for him. It was in her eyes. She would run soft fingers across him to soothe him, press her warm lips against him to excite him and do whatever he wanted anytime he wanted.

It was delicious and, for what felt hours, he gave in. Just let his mind switch off in the way it scarcely ever did as he embraced this strange ecstasy.

But thoughts of his sister kept returning to his mind, breaking his tranquillity, filling him with worry. She was in the house somewhere; he knew it, and he also knew he had to check she was okay. They had walked through the front door together. Just as they did everything together. They were each other's rock, so it was as impossible for him to abandon her as it would be for her to abandon him. If he was in the house, she would be too. And that being the case, he had to see her.

Still, as the anxiety rose, he found it hard to act on his concerns. The woman was on top of him; she was then underneath him. She was teaching him tricks even he'd never imagined. Since he was nineteen, he had enjoyed being between the thighs of beautiful, experienced, older women. But no one had ever been as insatiable as this woman. (Again, he struggled for her name. And once more the idea came forward finally that it was Tina. It seemed ungallant not to recall her name, but it also struck him she wouldn't be bothered. He had the insane idea that not only wouldn't she mind, but she'd find it sexy somehow.) Seemingly she possessed an extra pair of hands when she made love to him; her legs could grip him with an insane strength. Her pelvis squeezed and twisted against him to make him come with an incredible force he'd never experienced before.

The second they finished, she was ready to go again. An unbelievable carnality flashed instantly in her eyes, and he felt it too. He didn't even need space between couplings for his hardness to return, such was the effect this woman had on him, the inspiration she gave him. With her, he was permanently erect. He felt they could make love all day, into the night and right to a week next Tuesday without needing to take a break or have any kind of sustenance.

The first time he thought he would push himself away – make his excuses, promise (and mean it) that he'd return soon – a friend of hers arrived.

She literally walked into the bedroom wearing nothing but an old cowboy belt, with fake pistols and a Stetson tilted at an angle on her head. She was naked apart from these Calamity Jane accessories. Looking as if she'd wandered in from a very adult fancy dress party. This woman wasn't at all shy of her nudity, or bashful about interrupting them. Nor was Tina (it was Tina, wasn't it?) who invited her straightaway to join them. A lascivious smile filling her face. Well, this woman was as sexy as Tina. A little older, but with firm breasts, and dyed curly red hair the bright shade of liquorice swirls. He could not say no.

Where had these women been all his life? They were creatures of a thousand erotic fantasies. His chest heaved and his heart pounded and he felt giddy with the unremitting debauchery.

For a while, it was impossible to leave them. They banished all thoughts of Si from his mind. (What kind of man thinks of his sister in a sexual situation anyway?) Yet while the nagging worry could be muted, he couldn't let it go completely. And, despite the pauses between their passion being brief, there were pauses. Moments when he had to catch his breath, and the concern came back that he didn't know where his sister was, or whether she was safe. Neither of them knew if the other was okay.

Simone was out there, and thus he had to find her. Check in on her. He was sure she was fine. Simone was always fine, he was the one who needed looking after. But he still had to see her. Then he could come straight back and enjoy himself some more with his new friends. (The first one, he was sure, was called Tina. The second one he had no idea what she was called, but strangely he didn't feel bad about this.)

Gradually he inched himself from the bed. Surely it would be simple enough to articulate the words needed. Explain to them his task and promise he'd be gone only ten minutes. But the words didn't come. Somehow he knew if he said them out loud, it would turn into – if not an argument – then a good-natured debate. They'd reassure him Simone was fine, in a casual and breezy way which said he shouldn't worry so much. No doubt they'd tell him she was enjoying herself too. (How they'd know, he had no idea). They would say all of it with purring voices and lustful glances, then they'd position themselves tantalisingly around each other. It would be impossible to resist.

So instead he tried to slip quietly off the mattress, leaving them engaged with each other on the white (and apparently still stain-free) sheets. He hoped he'd be back before they really knew it. Obviously they'd miss him, but perhaps his being away for only five minutes would inspire them to new sexual heights when he returned.

The moment he stepped off the bed, however, it felt like something snapped. The atmosphere, which had been hot and sweaty, dropped several degrees. Standing naked on the bare floorboards, he shivered.

Tina had been lying on top of her friend, their breasts pressed together, kissing each other deeply. The instant he slid away, Tina sat up, her fringe fallen over her forehead, her eyes heavy with raw desire. Her friend turned to him as well, with the same unquenchable lust.

It was a fucking hot sight!

But it came with an unmissable sense of disappointment. Despite their ardent gazes, they were let down by him. There was sexual yearning, but he thought he could see – just at the edges – the beginnings of a cruel, unfathomable hatred.

They'd become women scorned only a few seconds

after he'd left their touch.

He knew, if he turned around and leapt onto the bed, that all would return to what it had been. (His erection had maintained itself, despite the temperature plummeting around him.) What he broke could be fixed. Their three bodies would roll around together and each of the ladies would scream loud as he fucked them. If he wanted it, he was sure Tina could rustle up another friend for him. It seemed nothing was off the table as far as she was concerned.

"Where are you going, lover?" she asked. Her voice low and drawling. Sex in audible form.

"I'm going to find Simone. Check she's okay. I'll be five minutes, ten tops. Keep yourselves warm." He chuckled. "We've got lots of fun ahead."

"Simone is fine," they spoke in unison. Not only did the words match, but so did their tones. Waving off his worries, they beckoned him to resume between the sheets.

Undoubtedly he was tempted, but he had already summoned the strength to take a step away. As he did, scowls filled their features, making them appear much more their actual ages. They glared at him. Desire remained apparent, but was now mixed with contempt. The memories of their fingers and tongues on him were warm and incredible, but his skin crawled and became clammy where they'd caressed him.

The trousers and shirt he'd been wearing were in a crumpled pile at his feet. He grabbed them up and wrestled them on clumsily, particularly as his phallus still rigidly pointed at them.

"Seriously," he said, talking to himself as much as them. "I do not want this to end. I am entranced by both you lovely ladies. But I have to check. Five minutes, that's all. Ten at most, since I don't really know my way around. Then I'll be back, my clothes will be off and…" He beamed at them, aware how devastatingly handsome he was with his cockiest smile. "Maybe when I'm gone, I can think of something new to try. Or you can. An act you've always wanted to perform. With you two, I'm ready for anything. But I need a few minutes first."

As he spoke, he trod backwards to the door, pretending he couldn't see the growing hatred on their faces. The image wasn't erotic anymore. It felt staged by two women old enough to know better, who didn't like each other much anyway and absolutely did not care for him.

He held both hands out to them and accompanying his smile with a wink. Hoping that five minutes would be all it was, and then he'd return and they'd make him cry with pleasure as he made them cry with pleasure.

His hand reached for the door handle. It was ice cold.

Not flinching or losing his composure in any way, he glanced at them, held up five fingers while with his other hand turned the handle. He then opened the door and disappeared through it.

Robin expected to be in the hallway.

Where else would he be?

The hallway had been the other side of the door.

But he wasn't in the grand old hall.

When he stepped through, he found himself in another sunlit bedroom, with another grand, four poster bed.

On the bed was a couple. They were fully dressed. The larger man with his arm around the smaller woman's shoulders. Robin's breath caught in his throat as he saw them.

It was Mark and Diane Costello. The couple he'd killed in the car crash long ago. Both regarding him with loathing.

CHAPTER TWENTY-SEVEN

It had been a spring morning.

He was nineteen.

Young and stupid.

He'd spent the night at a party. Most of his time that summer he spent at various parties. Drinking too much, consuming any substance which came his way, making passes at any remotely attractive girl he met. He was brash, rude and forced himself to the centre of everything. Back then, he told himself he made any party better. With the benefit of maturity, he saw he was callow and an utter show-off dick.

There was a pretty girl at the party. Elegant, one of the Sloan set from Chelsea. She wore a little black dress for a summer evening's event and had blonde hair in a perfect bob. They'd never met before and he only ever knew her nickname, but for most of the party she was his partner in crime, his enabler in crime. Sourcing some powder when everyone else claimed to have run short. Leading the charge – with him – into the wine cellar when all the above ground booze was consumed.

Of course, they retired to the first bedroom they could find. Sloppy kisses all the way. But once in there, his cocktail of blow, pot and booze threw him off his game and he was a distinct disappointment between the sheets. He tried his best with his hands, but it wasn't enough for her. Relations between them swiftly became frosty to the point of Antarctic. She rolled her eyes at him and announced she was going to find a man who "knew what the fuck he was doing."

But with everyone else comatose, or on the verge of unconsciousness, she was out of joy. And it filled him with a kind of malevolent glee to drive off in the Range Rover he'd borrowed for the night and leave her stranded. Waiting for someone else to wake up, or for the nearest taxi company to rouse a driver and send him out of the way to that stately pile.

He was laughing as he did it, even as he knew it was wrong to be driving. Stupid not to wait until he'd sobered a bit. Really, he could barely stand when he poured himself behind the wheel. Then he had to lower his head and squint through the dawn's light reflecting off the windshield.

However, his drive would only be ten minutes. To the farmhouse which his dissolute uncle called home in the middle of the countryside.

(In their hunt for a story after the accident, the press re-examined his uncle's shady business practices. He'd been investigated before, years earlier, and this was partly why he'd moved to such a remote location and hidden away. This time they dug deeper and found all manner of extra crimes which his uncle had committed. The police investigation was ongoing a year later when his uncle died. In his darkest nights, Robin added old, corrupt Uncle Bernard as another of his victims. Despite Si reminding him that the grumpy old git had made a start on drinking himself to death before anything else happened.)

Everything was a blur that morning, right until the accident happened. After the smash, all was frighteningly clear.

Suddenly he was at a blind corner. In his memory, he wasn't going particularly fast. A sensible part of him had yelled to his drunken mind that he needed to be careful. As far as he was concerned, he wasn't being reckless. It was a dreadful surprise then when a grey estate car approached from the other direction. He reassured himself he wasn't going too fast, but he couldn't get his foot on the brake or turn the wheel of the large four by four anywhere near quick enough. Before he really understood what was happening, he had shunted the other car off the road.

He didn't think he'd hit it with much force. It should have been a scrape and an exchanging of insurance details. But instead the other car spun away, half rising into the air before coming down heavy with a smash of glass and a crash of tortured metal. Landing on broken axels in a rivulet between the tarmac and a bramble hedge.

Robin's airbag deployed, trapping him, pinning him tight. But he could see everything over it. It meant he had no choice but to watch what happened next.

There was a couple in the front of the other car. The man was behind the wheel. When Robin stared at them, they both appeared to be swaying in the seats. The tremors of their landing reverberating through their bodies. They didn't move though, they just sat there. Absolute terror rising groggily onto their faces as the engine caught fire in front of them.

Robin's own head was woozy. The drugs and drink in play with the shock of the crash. But he was sure he called to them. Yelled at them to move.

But instead they sat there and waited to die.

Black smoke was billowing. Why didn't they move?

Later, he learned the accident had crushed in the front of their car. It trapped their legs beneath jagged, crunched metal. They literally could not move. Broken shards of steel pointed inwards, pinning down their thighs and leaving wide gashes in their flesh. Their blood splashed down into the seeping engine oil.

Right then, he felt only confusion. They weren't saving themselves. Why weren't they saving themselves? The fire was spreading from the front of the car. It was enveloping the entire vehicle. The flames were lapping at their skin.

He could hear their screams.

They stared at him the whole time. Just as he couldn't take his eyes off them, theirs were fixed on him.

In the many, many dark nights since, he'd tried to interpret their expressions. Fear absolutely, along with pain and dread. But was there also incomprehension at the fact he wasn't coming to help them? Or was it sheer hatred for what he'd managed so carelessly to do?

They died in front of him.

Trapped behind the airbag, he watched the fire consume them. Their hair burned from their scalps, their skin first blistering and then blackening. Even over the roaring flames, he could hear their final agonised shrieks.

It was more than ten minutes before another car came past. Closer to forty-five before a fire engine and ambulance made their way through the country lanes.

Far too late to save Mark and Diane Costello.

His family name – the fact his great grandfather had been somebody and his grandfather a lesser somebody – meant it hit the papers.

His and Simone's parents were already gone, so thankfully missed the scandal. But Si rushed back from Paris where she was studying.

Although it was obvious he had been in no condition to drive, the police botched the evidence. Losing the vital blood samples they'd taken.

That meant it went from accident to scandal on the front pages. He was the rich kid who could get away with anything – including manslaughter so careless, it was practically murder. He was the poster boy for pampered bastards everywhere. Despite the fact there was barely any money left in the family anymore.

Their solicitor – an old, well-mannered gent, who really should have been above such things – then made matters infinitely worse.

At first Robin hadn't wanted to learn the name of the couple who'd died. It would simply make it even more horrible and real. But then, with the strength of Si at his side, he wanted to find out everything about them. Mark and Diane Costello had been spending the night together in a tucked away country hotel. Only they weren't a married couple. They were a wife and her brother-in-law. She was married to his younger brother and the two were engaged in a torrid affair.

The solicitor leaked this salacious detail to a reporter, only he didn't disguise his steps well enough.

It exploded under them. Took off Robin's face in particular. The disgusting young toff trying to defame the deceased.

Free from police prosecution, but a figure of

contempt to both the press and the public, he retired to quietly have a nervous breakdown.

Si helped him through it. She had never stopped.

After a period holed up in a friend's house in London (where he met said friend's aunt for the first time), he and Si had then disappeared to Central America. There he waited for the world to turn and all the hatred written about him to transform into chip paper.

However, although the world did eventually forget, he could never forget. It was with him every day – and night.

He tried to make amends. Punishing those who had money, whose sins were planned rather than accidental. Genuinely giving a proportion of their earnings to charity so he could make the world better.

But now his two victims, the unfortunate Mark and Diane – who died a horrible death due to his recklessness – sat in front of him. Judging him.

CHAPTER TWENTY-EIGHT

They glared at him with the same expression they used in his most dreadful dreams. There was no pain or fear. Instead, their faces mirrored each other in hateful judgement. They fixed him not with hurt, but sheer and unending contempt.

Robin hadn't realised he'd got so far through the door for it to shut behind him, but it slammed – blown by a chilled breeze. His knees went weak and he felt at the precipice of bursting into tears. Becoming a frightened little boy in a man's body.

"Do you think of us?" Mark Costello asked, his voice low and croaky. A Dublin accent unmistakable. "Do you ever think of us and what you did?"

He was a big man, with a round belly and a bushy beard which bordered on the unkempt. His eyes were sad and tough. Like he constantly expected to be hurt. After the accident, when Robin had looked at photos of the man in supposedly happier times, he'd seen that his dourness was without end. At weddings and barbeques and birthday parties, his eyes showed no pleasure. Wherever he was, it didn't appear he wanted to be there. He was a large bloke forever in a stained jumper or a scruffy suit, the stereotype of a real ale drinker. But Robin imagined that when Mark Costello got started on the booze, he was a maudlin drunk.

Beside him, Diane Costello was utterly petite, to the point of girlish. No bigger than five foot and with an adolescent figure, her blonde hair having grown wild, so it brought to mind a teenager rebelling. In every photo Robin saw, she was eerily pale. As if she was constantly sick or hungry. There had been a ten year age gap between the two of them, but with him looking much older than he really was and her appearing much younger, it made them seem a lot more akin to father and daughter than wife and brother-in-law. Certainly no one would have cast them as lovers.

Her eyes were a big and watery blue, dominating her entire face. Expressive eyes, undoubtedly. And right then they were filled with righteous fury aimed at him.

"You've got over what happened to us, haven't you?" Her voice had flat estuary tones. "It's one of those things. Easy for *you* to move on, easy for *you* to continue living your life."

Robin's mouth opened. He wanted to defend himself, to make it clear he thought of them. There wasn't a day which passed when he wasn't racked by guilt for what had happened. He smiled, yes, and good times were undoubtedly had, but it never let go of him. He wanted to say this, make a declaration, but was it really enough to simply state out loud that he felt horrendously bad for inadvertently killing them?

"Look at him stood there," she continued. "His fancy ways, his life travelling around the world. All the money he's made so he could enjoy himself. I bet he laughs when he thinks of us. That he's one of those people who believes there are winners and losers, and we're the losers who got in his way."

"No!" Robin gasped. "That's not it!"

"Do you think of us?" Mark Costello asked more sternly.

He had his arm gripped around the slight shoulders of Diane. Fingers pressing bruises into her delicate skin. She leant into him, her own arms tight and defensive across her chest.

"I *do* think of you!" Robin wanted to stay composed, but realised he was practically shrieking. "Every day. Every hour. I wish things didn't happen the way they did. That I was a minute later, or a minute earlier and we just passed each other on the road and thought no more about it. I wish I'd never fucking got behind the wheel of that car."

The scorn on Diane's face showed she didn't believe a single syllable he uttered.

"It's true!" he cried. "I'm sorry for what happened. Totally and completely sorry. I've hated myself for it, tortured myself for it."

"Bullshit!" she snapped. Her expression pinched, her voice full of disdain.

"When?" asked Mark Costello.

"Yes, when?" she demanded. "When have you tortured yourself? Was it when you were flying first class? When you were checking into expensive hotels? Drinking champagne at parties? Was it when you were seducing old ladies? Or counting the zeroes in your bank balance? When the fuck did you torture yourself about what happened to us?"

He felt trapped. "I did!" he protested, his voice much higher, pleading and whining at once. "I tried to make amends for it. I tried to punish people in the way…"

"In the way you should have been punished?" she growled.

Feebly, he nodded. "I went after absolute bastards. Villains and scum. I've tried to hurt them, to hit them in their wallets – the thing they care for most – so that I did some good for the world. Paid back a little karma."

"A right Robin Hood, aren't you?" she sneered.

Mark Costello's dark countenance was obviously unimpressed. "Similar to Diane, I'm not sure I fully understand. Are you saying by taking money from people who can easily afford it, you make up for our screaming incineration?"

There was no way he could answer the question satisfactorily. He shook his head, helpless.

"A good part of the money goes to charity," he said weakly, knowing he was damning himself. "Not as much as should, but I try. There are costs to finance what we do. Frequently we have to move on. It isn't cheap. But I still fund good causes." He risked a glance at Mark. "You ran a marathon for an Irish cancer charity, didn't you? *They've* had donations from me." Then to Diane. "And you supported the lifeboats. That was on your Facebook page, your Amigo page too. I made sure money went to them as well. And orphans," he said desperately. "My sister and I were orphaned at a young age."

"But after costs?" she snarled. "We know where you've been and we honestly cannot conceive how the finest hotel in the Napa Valley and dinner at The French Laundry count as legitimate costs."

"I did my best!" he wailed. Knowing he hadn't,

aware he could have done much more. Suddenly he was weak at the knees, liable to pitch forward.

"You lived your life!" Diane yelled at him. "That's what you did! You lived the life you wanted, an immoral and disreputable life, then convinced yourself you were a good man doing the right thing. Claimed it was in our memory. What about your sister? What of her life? A lesbian encouraged to make eyes at men more than twice her age, so she can make you feel worthwhile about yourself."

"No. She supports me." Then added quickly: "We support each other."

"When do you support her?" Mark asked with a sniff. "As far as I can see, you do nothing for anybody who isn't yourself."

"I've tried!" Robin was sobbing. "Those bastards I dealt with had done bad things. The courts couldn't touch them and I made sure they got some kind of punishment. Si and I did it together."

Diane Costello's eyes blazed. "*You* did bad things and the courts couldn't touch *you*! Where is your fucking punishment? What has your sister done to be sentenced to life looking after such worthless filth as you?"

"Do you know the name of the lady your sister is currently courting?" Mark asked. The plain, matter-of-fact tone of his voice making it crueller.

Si had told him of her. She was a teacher. Shy, apparently. Her name had been mentioned, but he couldn't recall it. It wouldn't come to him right then, and he hated himself for that.

A glance passed between the two of them on the bed. One which suggested he'd sunk further than even their base expectations.

Mark Costello coughed through his big, furry beard. "Do you seriously think you've done good works with your life? Do you consider you've gone any way to rectify for what you did to us?"

"Yes. Do you?" she snarled.

All words had fled. He couldn't bring himself to repeat "I tried". He knew how pathetic and worthless it would sound.

"*Do you?*" she yelled.

But then the atmosphere altered. They weren't looking at him; they were peering past him. Dimly he was aware the door behind him had opened. His first impulse was to turn and run to Tina and friend. They'd welcome him and would do such things to him, that they'd make it seem like this awful confrontation never happened. It would wipe the whole episode from his mind, replace it with blissfully tangled limbs and satisfied sighs. But he also knew eroticism was beyond him at that instant. All he wanted was to weep.

He needed to find Simone.

There was a fragment of hope that – although he knew it to be illusionary the second it leapt into his breast – it was her who had walked through the door.

When he turned, all air caught cold in his chest. Standing before him was Belinda.

There was dripping blood and vivid bruises across her face. It had been brutally beaten in.

"YOU did this to me!"

CHAPTER TWENTY-NINE

"No!"

Robin staggered. Unable to comprehend.

Yes, it was Belinda. She stood in front of him, he could smell a strange, sour sweat which came off her, but surely this had to be an apparition. She couldn't really be there. Nothing bad could have happened to her.

He enjoyed this woman. The time they'd spend together was fun. Genuinely, he thought that. The initial point had been to get her money, but he surprised himself by falling a little for her. Some of what had been written about her was undoubtedly true, but a lot of it wasn't. It was obviously the case her husband had been the main bastard in their relationship, even if she hadn't painted a pretty picture of herself after he died. But person-to-person and face-to-face, she was vibrant, as well as incredibly exciting in bed. He hadn't felt bad about ripping her off, but he'd also greatly looked forward to spending time with her.

What they had together was a beautiful bubble. She'd met Si once, but she knew nothing else of the rest of his life and he was sure she wouldn't have followed him around. There was no reason she'd be in Breakspear Hall. She couldn't be there. Not looking so hurt and broken, she couldn't! It was all fantasy, not reality.

A thousand arguments against what he was seeing spun around his mind, but the truth settled heavy into his core. She was an apparition, a ghost come to haunt him. Somehow, tragically, she'd died since he'd last seen her. And – horribly – it was once again his fault.

"*You* did this to me!" The first word was a guttural roar from the depths of her throat. She stepped forward, making sure he got a good look at the crimson swelling of skin, as well as the broken capillaries behind her eyes. Her jaw moved heavily behind swollen lips. He could see the black gaps of missing teeth in there.

Quivering, he backed away, hands held up defensively in front of him. Behind him were the Costellos, so he knew he couldn't go far, but nor could he stand firm in the face of her advance. Her anger was too much to bear.

"The man who beat me did so because of you." Her words slurred. "He came after the money you took! He punished me because I was soft-hearted to you! Because I believed the lies you told me!"

At the last word, she choked. Her mouth opened wider and her face turned an uglier purple. With a wheeze, she doubled at the waist and coughed. Then, with a kind of reverse swallow, she spat something onto the floorboards.

Robin stared down at it, eyes wide in disbelief. It was a finger. She had regurgitated a little finger. Grey and severed from a human hand.

"I don't know how that got there," the thing which used to be Belinda croaked. "I must speak to my niece about it. She died because of *you* as well!"

"No!" he whimpered. He wanted to deny the charge, but knew he couldn't voice any words which claimed it wasn't his fault. The mere fact she was there, told him it was his responsibility. He didn't know how or what had happened, but what she was saying was as true as when Mark and Diane Costello had made their accusation. He was responsible for Belinda's death.

"With my last breaths," she said, taking another step forward. "I reached with love for you. Hoping my heart would sense yours and I'd know it was worth it. I might have died, but I'd had the love of a good man. Finally, a decent man. But do you know what?" Her voice rose. "There was nothing! Nothing at all! You didn't love me the way I loved you. You didn't care for me the way I cared for you. I was another old dame to be played around with, another heart to be broken. One with a few more trinkets to squander on you, but it was the same fucking drill as always, wasn't it, Robin?"

"I did really like you!" he cried. The moment the words left his lips, he knew how pathetic they sounded.

"*Like?*" It had more force than just her voice. An angry choir seemed to burst forth around it. The noise echoed not only around the room, but the house itself. "Like? Is that all it was? Nothing more. No love, no great affection. In another six months, would you have remembered my name?"

Of course he would. But he couldn't honestly swear in six months' time she'd have had a working mobile number for him. And what kind of compensation was it, really, if he could remember her name?

"I loved you!" she screamed. "Don't you understand that? Right down into my soul. Yet when my love rose to meet yours, there was nothing! I realised at the end that not only did I love you, but I was literally going to die for you. Yet to you, I was nothing. Depressingly disposable. A busty cow with cellulite and a large bank balance, who you could fleece for a couple of hundred grand, before moving on to the next one. That was it, wasn't it?"

"I-I-I." He tried, but there were no words.

"I died because of you," she cried. "I was murdered and my niece was murdered and it was all because of your actions. And you didn't give the slightest fuck about me, or tell me anything but lies the entire time we were together. You didn't like me, you merely liked the zeroes in my bank account!"

"No. I did."

"I mentioned my niece to you, didn't I? What was her name?" she challenged.

In any other circumstance, Robin would have wagered on remembering the name. Given his profession, recall was extremely useful. Now, however, the shock of it all had left him numb. His mind scrambled fruitlessly.

Si's new girlfriend and Belinda's niece. Two women he'd been told of, but couldn't remember the most basic element of what had been said. What kind of confidence man was he?

"See!" she howled. "That's how little interest you took in me. I died for you. My beautiful young niece died for you. And you do not care!"

"He simply lives his life and doesn't mind who he hurts." Diane Costello jeered from behind him.

Spinning on his heel, he stared at them on the bed and then back to Belinda, who was advancing towards him. In the blur of motion which was his whiplashed gaze, he spotted a door at the other side of the room. When he started running, he wouldn't have sworn it was real. It might have been a woozy apparition. But he went anyway. His toes kicking into the floorboards and sprinting. His lungs screaming the entire way.

CHAPTER THIRTY

Breakspear led, holding off his impossible-to-disguise dodderiness as he rushed through the winding mess of corridors. Through doorways whose positions seemed to shift before her eyes; down passageways which, for her, repeated over and over. The same wallpaper, the same damp in the same corners of the ceilings. On her own, she would have been lost upstairs for decades. He though had spent most of his life exploring these rooms, learning the tricks the house might play, understanding how to get past them.

When he led them onto the top landing, there appeared to be actual daylight outside. The windows within Breakspear Hall were themselves deceitful. Already she'd seen so many shades of light and darkness. This however felt real, the dawn at the end of an extremely long night.

Breakspear rested a trembling hand on the bannister. Wincing, she knew she wouldn't have done it. The wood was old and rotting. She could almost see the woodworm crawling throughout. The polished shine which had greeted them when they first walked in was rubbed away. But Breakspear grabbed on tight, with the confidence of a man who had long been protected by this house.

The opulence of the hallway had vanished. Every sense of wealth and taste had proved illusionary. There were no wood panels anymore and no portraits. The carpet was not so lush you could feel its warmth beneath the soles of your shoes. Instead, the floorboards were rotting; some had cracked, leaving dark holes underneath. One wrong step would not see you plunge into the cellar, but into an infinitely worse place far below. In the morning light, the walls were grey, bare and damp. Stripped to brick and crumbling. Whatever the masonry equivalent of wood worm was, those creatures were gorging themselves.

Robin was at centre of the hallway, dressed in blood-stained and dusty clothes. He was wailing at the aged blistered ceiling. More distraught than he had been after the accident, or following their mother's death a few months after their father's.

At the stairs, Breakspear didn't hesitate, bounding down two at a time. She was more cautious, going as fast as she could while making sure of every footfall. There was no way she wanted to tumble and snap her neck when she was so close to her brother. So near to getting the hell out of there.

On the ground floor, Breakspear slowed and allowed her to get ahead of him. Obviously offering comfort to her brother was not his place. She dropped to her knees and wrapped her arms around Robin. Cradling him and feeling the sobs cascade through his body.

Breakspear stared around the hallway and then

down at the siblings, his eyes narrowed. "We have to get him a long way distant from here!" His baritone rumbled around the big, empty space.

There was no way of getting through to Robin. He knew she was there; he clung to her as he always did in times of need. But the sounds of his crying drowned her words. He'd hear the soothing and love within them, but not what she was saying. It was years since she'd last seen him as bad as this. Time healed, even the worst things. His most awful dreams these days did not leave him racked with such sorrow, only regret. He was clinging to her, taking her support. But she couldn't lift him and march him out, no matter how much she wanted to.

Every thirty seconds he raised his head to glance at the doorway second right beyond the stairs. There was nothing she could see there, but when he took a deep breath in between sobs, she could hear the faint echo of voices purring his name. Female and flirtatious, gasping "Robin" with anticipatory delight. It was a Siren's call which made her shudder.

She knew she had to calm him first.

"What happened?" Simone asked. Hands stroking through his hair, trying to quieten him enough so he'd listen. "Tell me what the hell happened."

Above her, fury creased into Breakspear's face. His glare fixed on the other side of the hallway. The man – or whatever he was – had not come the same way they had, but Murkiss had joined them.

Pressing Robin's head to her breast, she felt her own heartbeat echo. It got faster with the urgency of the moment.

"Please talk to me, Robin," she whispered. "Tell me what's wrong. Tell me what happened."

"I killed her!" he cried, his voice a tear-filled rasp.

She was all too familiar with his self-hatred after one of his nightmares, but then he normally cried that he'd killed *them*.

"Killed who?" she asked.

"Belinda," he gasped. "I killed Belinda."

The surprise was so great she spoke without thinking. "The little man outside the casino. He said he was after Belinda's money. That we'd taken it from her."

Robin pulled back from her, nearly slumping to the floor. She only just held onto him. "What man?"

Her jaw clenched. "The one who attacked me with the knife."

She clutched her arms tighter around him even before the howl came. His entire body heaved, and she thought he would be sick, or that he might hyperventilate until he passed out.

Breakspear was right beside her, unable to hide his impatience. "We don't have time for this. We really have to go. I have to get the two of you off the estate. Not merely from the house, but in a taxicab on the main road away from here. Young man!" he called.

His voice boomed, but Robin was too lost in dark emotions to listen.

"You have to get up!" Breakspear barked in irritation. "Pay no attention to those far-off chants. Do not take the easy way. Instead, stand like a man and walk towards the door!"

"Come on, Robin," she urged in a more caring whisper. "Let's get you up."

Caught in his cries of pain, he didn't hear. Or didn't want to hear. He might not move until the anguish had bored itself in deep.

Again those cooing voices came. It annoyed her that he had the urge to respond to them in a way he wasn't responding to her.

"Please!" yelled Breakspear. "You need to understand that time is of the essence. We don't know how long we may have."

As loud as he was, Robin didn't seem to hear him. However, his words jammed in Simone's mind. She must get Robin out.

But then another voice spoke, soft and unctuous, yet somehow making itself heard where Simone and Breakspear failed.

"Mr Robin, sir," Murkiss said, taking a deferential step towards the three of them. "I do hate to raise this in polite company, but Miss Tina and her friend have asked me to pass on a message." He coughed once, as if approaching a delicate subject. "They wanted me to say they are missing you and are eager for your undivided attention once more."

The distant voices laughed blissfully.

Suddenly Robin stopped screaming. Instead, he held his gaze level towards the butler. Did the man frighten him as much as he did her? Or was it something else? She realised Robin hadn't stopped crying because the man disturbed him, but because he was listening to what he said. His words were a kind of opiate.

"No!" Breakspear roared. He stepped between the two of them, blocking Robin's sight of Murkiss. "You already have me, you don't need anyone else. Do not speak to him, do not sink your claws into him! I am enough for you and I can last a few good years yet, and you damn well know it."

Robin glanced at her, confused. Despite the man's

forceful interjections, it appeared to be the first time he'd properly noticed the supposed master of the house.

"It's Breakspear," she whispered.

Robin's eyes widened momentarily in confusion, but then came acceptance. Who could tell what else he had already seen in this house?

Breakspear had stiffened himself in high dudgeon, shoulders thrown back. He seemed like a tall, resolute rock. "You do not listen to him, young man," he said, never taking his eyes off the butler. "You have your faults, I'm sure of that, but you do not deserve this fate. Get up, walk towards the front door and keep going. Think of yourself as the wife of Lot. Whatever you do, don't turn around."

"I really think Mr Robin can make his own decision, sir." Not once was Murkiss's voice anything other than measured and respectful.

"No!" Breakspear bellowed. The echo crumbling some of the brickwork. "You have me! This will end with me, do you hear? I am the last of the Breakspears. The last member of this accursed line and nothing you can do will change it. This all ends with me!"

Taking a step from the butler, he bent down and grabbed Robin by the elbow, trying to haul him to his feet. Still on her knees, Simone did her bit to help from the other side. But her brother – although he wasn't crying anymore – seemed to have made himself deliberately heavy. It was as if he didn't want to be saved.

"Come on!" she gasped.

There was a polite cough, one which sent a shiver through her every nerve-ending.

"Ahem," murmured Murkiss. "You are of course

aware that you've already named an heir, aren't you, sir?"

The speed with which Breakspear snapped up his neck and glared at the odious man disturbed the air. "*What?*" An explosion of shock in one syllable.

It happened too quickly. Breakspear dropped Robin's arm, let it slip from his fingers. Then he stood tall. Only this time he was nowhere near as powerful, a pained grimace carved deep into his face. His skin turned white. He wasn't aging to an old man once more, but it was clear all life was draining from his body. Feebly, he lifted his trembling right arm, clutching it across his chest. And then Montagu Breakspear's eyes rolled into his head and he dropped face first to the floor. The echo of the impact rebounding around the cavernous hall.

"No!" cried Robin, roused from his stupor by the sight of another fatality.

Simone stayed on her knees, paralysed. She watched as her brother turned over the body and then his fists pounded Breakspear's chest, but she knew it was hopeless. There was nothing either of them could do.

With a tremor, she realised how close behind her Murkiss skulked. She could smell him. It was as cloying as old boiled sweets in a forgotten tin.

His aspect was as outwardly pleasant as always. "I hope this won't be deemed inappropriate, Miss Simone, given how we're still coming to terms with the recent tragic passing." He glanced toward Breakspear's corpse, Robin still attempting to beat life into him. "But I wanted to be the first to congratulate you on becoming the new mistress of Breakspear Hall."

CHAPTER THIRTY-ONE

Robin continued to pound in vain at Breakspear's sunken chest. Her brother's-kneeling form concealed Breakspear's face, but to her he appeared a very old man, shrivelled before her eyes. Surely Robin realised it was hopeless, but he kept going. Desperate, after everything, to save someone.

Beside him, she stayed silent and felt numb. Outside it was daylight, she was sure it was really dawn, but the space around her was dark. A tight little box which was gradually closing in on her. The lid slammed and nails hammered in. Around her, the house itself was shifting, its architecture altering and growing. Her vision blurred as she tried to determine her path towards the front door and, for a few seconds, all around was whirling. The door was no longer a fixed point, but was instead going up and down and would be wherever she wasn't.

Maybe she would have fainted right then. She'd never swooned as an adult, but surely this was the perfect time. But Robin's fury beside her gave her something else to focus on. She turned her head and watched him, not saying a word, but concentrating on his effort and wondering if she herself would ever move again.

Of course, the butler was already right behind her. She knew he would always be behind her from this hour on, and it might be the worst element of this fate.

"I don't understand," she muttered, her voice flat, sounding distant to herself. "It's not mine, he didn't leave it to me."

"Oh, but he did, Miss Simone. Don't you remember?" asked Murkiss. "Mr Breakspear informed you he was happy for you to have everything of his. That you could take it all, I think was his wording."

The echo of his words screeched through her mind.

"*You want my money? Only money? You can have it! You can take it all for the good it will do you in this place.*"

She remembered the gruesome, hysterical laughter which accompanied the dark jibe.

"But, no, that wasn't it." Still she hadn't stirred, her voice speaking from inside the most dreadful dream. "He wasn't being serious. He was only *joking*."

Murkiss's tone was as polite as always, but she could hear the syrupy bastard was enjoying himself. "It can often be hard to judge the full import of what someone is saying. An inflexion can be misinterpreted. The tone might not be apparent to a recent acquaintance who doesn't know the speaker so well. However, I was fortunate enough to be acquainted with Mr Breakspear for a very long time. More years than either of us would wish to calculate, I'm sure. And I am completely confident, as are my cohorts, he meant what he said. Indeed, when he uttered those words, he was making a solemn vow."

He had waved his hand, she noticed, when he said cohorts. It was as if he was including others who stood next to him. For a flickering instant she glimpsed faces in the walls, hundreds of them.

"No." She shook her head to get the image from her mind, squeezed her eyes tight to pretend she never saw it. "This cannot be right. It would never stand up in a court of law."

Beside her, Robin was starting to surrender. His face puce from effort. There was nothing he could do, and he was beginning to admit it to himself. With a last push, he yelled out loud, then dropped backwards. His hand pushing through his hair as he tried to grasp his breath.

Murkiss chortled. "I'm not sure this is a case which will ever make its way to the civil courts. Besides, those bodies have little sway here. As you heard the late Mr Breakspear say, there are no other claimants. No distant relatives who will come along and query your right to inherit. The house is yours, Miss Simone."

The words were slow to penetrate her, but Robin picked up on them much faster. He gawped at her and then the butler. "What the fuck is going on, Si?"

She ignored him, holding her gaze on Murkiss, her breath icy in her chest. "You don't want me. You don't want a woman in residence here. Breakspear told me."

His bald pate shone strangely as he nodded, the daylight seeming to both reflect from and pierce his pink skin. "It will pose challenges, I'm sure, Miss Simone. But challenges are a part of existence. What we need is someone young and healthy, whose energy we can draw on and who we can reward handsomely. I'm sure, as time passes, we'll find a way to offer you the pleasure you require." He chuckled to himself.

"And who knows what the fates may bring? Perhaps with you here we will achieve what has eluded us thus far. A proper heir, a child in your womb. The walls of Breakspear echoing with young, guileless laughter for the first time in far too long."

Vomit bubbled into her mouth and she only just swallowed it back down.

Robin clutched hold of her arm. "What the hell is he talking about, Si?"

The words, when they came, were a breathless whisper. "He says this house is mine."

"What? That's not right. You don't want this house, *we* don't want this house" He stared fearfully at the big front door they'd walked through earlier.

It was left to Murkiss to answer his points. "I'm afraid what Miss Simone wants is no longer relevant, Mr Robin. The undeniable truth is dear old Mr Breakspear left the house to her, a promise made in front of many witnesses. Undoubtedly gratitude to you for having saved his life played a large part in his decision. It was incredibly generous of him, don't you think?"

He beamed at Simone, apparently believing she'd nod in agreement.

Instead, she shook. Spasms taking her arms and then her legs. Her whole body on the verge of convulsing. "I want to go!" she cried. "I want to get out of here!"

Thankfully, Robin didn't argue. Now it was her who needed help, he didn't fold into himself, but actually moved. He took her arm (his own hand shaking, she noticed) and pulled her up in the direction of the door. All she could hope was he saw it a lot clearer than she did.

"But please," said Murkiss, mollifying behind them. "This house needs you, we all need you. I'm afraid you haven't seen the place at its best yet. This is a house for a young man – or a young lady – as when it has youth, it is a vibrant home. Mr Breakspear was old. He could no longer provide the sense of life to this place he should have. With you here, well, all will be different."

Ignoring him, Robin circled his arm around her waist and pushed her forward. She clutched onto him. He would need support too. They glanced at each other. Brother and sister who'd always resembled each other in good looks, perfect smiles and confidence. Now that resemblance was gritted teeth and fear.

Two steps was all they took. Then the earthquake consumed them.

The floor shook violently, testing their already trembling legs. Around them the walls bowed, bending inwards, seeking to prod them. From above, the ceiling creaked, sounding on the verge of collapse.

They stopped, clutching each other tight. A hopeless cry escaped her.

The instant they stopped moving forward, the house settled back into itself. Everything became solid. But that didn't mean things were the way they should be. Not in Breakspear Hall.

Simone saw it first. She reared upwards and it was there where the walls met the ceiling in a ninety-degree angle. Something was seeping. A thick, dark goo.

It couldn't be, could it?

Her eyes widened until she was sure she was actually seeing it. When the house shook, it had opened old wounds. Slashes in the infrastructure which were barely sealed. Those wounds were bleeding. Blood was running down the surrounding walls.

Robin gasped too. That gave her a brief flicker of relief. He'd wobbled on the floorboards, but in his silence she didn't know if he was witnessing all she saw. If the house was showing him the same things as her. But the horror in his expression was unmissable.

"I'm afraid it's difficult for you to leave, Miss Simone." Murkiss had crept behind them. "It's not impossible, of course, if you really want to, but I'm afraid I will have to come with you. In many ways, the house will have to come with you too. It needs a youthful energy and, when you're away, it makes it much harder to draw it from you. The process will be much more," he hesitated for the right word, "taxing for you. It's better if you stay here. Enjoy yourself. Let the house replenish, give some time for you and she to learn how to appreciate each other. That's the way I think you should go, Miss Simone. As a sudden exit, I feel, will be painful for all concerned."

Emphasising the butler's point, the house darkened. If she stared, she could see light through the crescent window, but it was as if someone had pulled a shade shut on the reality beyond. The house proving to her, Murkiss proving to her, that should she disobey it would literally switch her lights off.

But fuck it, she thought.

Within the walls, she saw a thousand faces loom towards her. Shaping themselves from the brickwork. Hard visages with snarling jaws. They watched her with judgemental eyes, ready to scream if she ventured another inch forward.

Still, she kept her shoulders straight.

Let it do its worse. She'd worry about it later. She'd happily worry about it in ten minutes' time if it meant she was out of this damn building and off this property.

Her arm clutching her brother, she jerked forward, only to find he was resisting.

"What are you doing?" she gasped, panicked

"No." He stood still. "We have to stop."

CHAPTER THIRTY-TWO

"What are you doing?" she repeated. "We have to leave!"

Even as the words burst from her lips, the house trembled. Anywhere else she'd imagine those old bricks would disintegrate. Not Breakspear Hall. She suspected it would always be there.

Robin didn't answer her, instead he glanced at the butler. A spotless impersonation of elegance in this decaying hallway. "What is this place? What's happening to us?"

"This is Miss Simone's home," replied Murkiss. Stating a self-evident fact.

"No," Robin started to say something else, but seemed to mislay his words.

"This is a house which hates to be empty," Murkiss continued. "It needs company, it needs youth. It is a very special house." He beamed with pride.

Simone watched as Robin regarded the hallway again. He gasped. Staring around the big space in wonder, as if for him it was transforming into a wonderful sight.

"What's happening?" he asked in a whisper.

Murkiss took a step closer, his voice confidential. "I know you found solace here, Mr Robin. New friends. That you did – ahem – enjoy yourself. But I'm sure, as Miss Simone's brother, she will let you stay. An honoured guest."

The words roused Simone. "Don't do that!" She stepped forward herself. "Don't speak to him."

"If I have spoken carelessly, then I apologise," Murkiss said quickly. "I naturally assumed, since you are siblings and such close siblings, an offer of accommodation would be forthcoming to your brother. It was the great regret of my time here with the two younger Mr Breakspears, that I couldn't make them connect more to other people."

"What is this place?" asked Robin. His eyes wide.

What was he seeing here? What illusion was the house affording him?

Simone tugged urgently at his arm. It seemed to work, Robin shook his head and peered down at her.

"Come on!" she ordered. "The door is there. This time we're going through it."

"The house is yours, Miss Simone!" tootled Murkiss. "It's not a building which enjoys being empty and, as such, I feel you will have great trouble leaving it."

"I don't want it!"

"Mr Breakspear's bequest was perfectly clear. All he had was yours. His principal asset, his only asset really, was lovely, old Breakspear Hall."

"But you don't want me!" she screamed at him. Robin wasn't moving. She tugged at his arm, but the stupid bastard wasn't moving. "Just let me be. Find somebody else."

"What would happen if I were to walk out of here without Simone?" Robin asked, his voice an oddly calm contrast to hers.

"It's you it's after," she said to him. "It wants men here, not women."

Murkiss ignored her. "The choice is yours, quite obviously, Mr Robin. But I think the house has taken to you. If you were to stay, at Miss Simone's invitation, then you would have a fine time here. Not only would it delight Miss Tina to see you, but I'm sure her friends would be overjoyed as well. In fact, they are waiting for you, sir."

"Don't listen to him!" Simone cried.

"But I could," Robin said, still fixed on Murkiss, "if I wanted to, just walk out of here? If I tried that, the walls wouldn't seem to be falling in, there wouldn't be cries at the distance. It would look as it does now."

How did it look to him? What was he seeing?

"Of course, sir," said Murkiss, pleasantly. "The choice is entirely yours."

As a very young child, she could remember stamping her feet to get her own way in arguments with her parents. She nearly did the same right then to her brother. "Don't listen to him!" she repeated. "We'll go together, I don't care what horrors it shows me, I don't give a fuck what happens outside, I want to leave."

"I'm afraid as owner," Murkiss told her, "you wouldn't survive very well out there if you left and attempted not to return. It requires energy to run a place as beautiful as this, and the farther the distance, the more energy is required. Better to stay here," he said cheerfully. "I'm sure you and the house will soon get used to each other."

As beautiful as this? A mouldy old pile of bricks being eaten from the inside? But that's what she was seeing, it was obvious Robin was looking at a different, more enticing house. An attractive home.

"I don't want to stay!" she cried. "I'd rather die!"

"Now, Miss, you don't mean that. I know you're being melodramatic for effect. Women are more prone to hysteria than men." He pursed his lips. "It may take a short time, but I'm sure you will find pleasure here."

Once again she grabbed at Robin. Attempted to yank him from this repellent creature. He continued not to move.

"So if Si was to leave, she'd die?"

"Not immediately, sir. But she would age before her time. It would be painful for her out there."

"And if she stayed?"

"Then the house would be hers and she would enjoy herself. Her proclivities are such," he bowed his head a touch in embarrassment, "maybe she and the house would be a good fit for each other. After all, we are highly experienced at providing our masters with lovely ladies to pass the time."

"You can't bribe me with sex!" she yelled. Outraged that she was being discussed as a distant stranger.

Again she pulled at her brother's arm, and again he stayed firmly rooted.

"What if I was the owner?" Robin asked.

"What?" The exclamation came as much to herself as to him.

"Answer me the question." He held Murkiss's full attention. "What if I became the owner? Simone said it would be better for you if a man took possession. If she were to transfer ownership to me, would that make you happy? More importantly, could she then leave?"

"Stop talking!" she yelled. "No!"

Thin lipped and pliant, Murkiss smiled. "I think it would be a very equitable solution, Mr Robin."

"No!" she repeated. "You can't do this! I won't give it to you!"

He turned and held her by the shoulders. "Please. Simone. I will not leave you. But you *can* leave me. You can live your life. I deserve this place. You don't."

There were tears flooding her vision. Her words came thick with hurt. "We stick together!"

"Not today. Now, I *need* to stay here. After what happened to the Costellos…"

"That was nearly ten years ago. You've tried to make amends."

"But it's with me, Si. Every day. You know that better than anyone." The resolve which had come across him was cracking at the edges, his own voice wavering. "With Belinda added in as well, I've too much on my shoulders. I can't leave this place. I can't pretend nothing happened. But I can't stay and watch this house eat you. Especially as you wouldn't be here if it wasn't for me."

"You can't!" She shook her head. "I won't let you."

"I have to do it. And I want you to go. I'll stay here, but I will leave eventually. I promise you. Breakspear went to his casino, after all. I will come and find you." He tried for a smile, but failed. "It won't be until a little time in the future, I'm sure, but eventually I'll come and meet you. We'll be together. But for now, I have to be here and you really, really don't."

"I won't do it!" she cried. "I won't."

It was then the house responded. A scream of a thousand voices burst from an unfathomably deep basement. The crumbling brickwork was shaken further, but not enough to collapse. Never enough to truly damage it. Those voices screamed her name with a mixture of hatred and dark craving.

Again she saw the faces in the wall. A thousand men from generations past, snarling at her with damnation and venom. She wasn't all a woman should be; she wasn't wanted within those walls. If she didn't do what the house desired, then the faces of those men would take immense satisfaction from screaming their hatred of her for every hour of eternity.

In a mere few seconds, Simone saw her future in this house. Most of the time numb and alone, wandering the hallways and avoiding Murkiss's condescension. Occasionally letting herself surrender to the temptations on offer, but knowing it would be an empty physical sensation from which she'd derive no pleasure. Her entire soul would close forever. She'd experience no hope or love or a semblance of happiness. Years would pass and she'd be the loneliest individual in the universe.

Until the incredibly dark day, the house itself would fill her womb. She wouldn't know how it happened – couldn't comprehend of how it might happen – but one day she'd realise she was pregnant. A baby inside her. Half her and half Breakspear Hall. A son which would eat her whole as soon as it was born, if it didn't consume her from the inside first.

The house showed her those stark flashes of what would transpire if she didn't leave. Robin would be there somewhere. He wouldn't desert her, but they'd still be lost to each other. Both trapped in their separate vortexes of numbness and pain. He'd shred his youth in the arms of a thousand imaginary women, while his own soul was ground to nothing.

It was all there for a few seconds. Her future played out in sharp images and deafening sounds.

"No!" she cried. "No, I can't."

Then she met the pleading eyes of her brother. He wanted to stay; the house wanted him more. If she was stubborn and remained, he'd be here anyway. But if she left, he'd have something to aim for. A reason to try to free himself from the confines. There was a chance he could get away, wasn't there? A slim chance, but it was there.

"Simone," he whispered.

They were children once more. He could almost have been peering up at her, asking for a favour, or the last slice of cake, or for her to smooth things over once more between him and Dad. She might be spiteful and make him wait, but she'd never been able to resist him.

"Okay," she said. "You can have it. Dear God, you can have it! I give it to you."

And with that, everything became still. The echo of the noise faded. The images shimmered to nothing, little more than daydreams.

"A wise choice, Miss Simone," Murkiss's voice said. "Thank you."

She turned her head in his direction, but he had gone too.

CHAPTER THIRTY-THREE

All of a sudden the house felt warm. Dawn's light came unfiltered through the crescent window and wood panelling grew up the walls, an eerily efficient plant. Underneath she could see the bricks were replenishing themselves.

It hadn't wanted Simone, but Robin it would look after.

Her brother stared at her, their hands gripped together. This time when he went for a smile, he managed it. There was something new in his eyes. She had long ago got used to the sadness there, to an anger at the world and the consequences of his actions within it. But now she thought there was a resignation, an acceptance. He could almost have appeared peaceful, but how could he be peaceful in a house like this?

"I could stay with you," she said. "You shouldn't be alone here."

"You have to go."

"I don't want to."

"Si, you have to. I make the decisions, remember?"

She nearly responded with 'it's a partnership', but this felt so untrue she wouldn't be able to stop the tears. "You'll be trapped. You didn't speak to Breakspear, you don't know what will happen to you here."

"I'll be okay. It will be a well-appointed jail. There was always a risk I might end my career in a cushy open plan prison, but instead I'm here."

"This is a prison with no release date."

"I'm resourceful."

She squeezed her fingers tighter around his. "So you always claim."

"I'll find a way. If anyone can, it's me. You know it! You need to trust me more." He leant in and kissed her softly on the cheek, his lips cold. "You've done more than any big sister should be asked to do. You've been a boulder for me, but I've been reliant on you for too long. I have held you back, stopped you living the life you should have. What was that teacher's name?"

"Lizzie," she murmured.

"Go to her. Go to someone else. Just find a way to be happy."

"I can't leave you here."

"I'm a selfish person, Si. Don't be loyal and try to defend me. I've done bad things, I've caused bad things to happen. I've," – he struggled to say the word – "killed people. I'm what Dad used to call bad news. Remember, he more than once said that if I wasn't careful I'd grow up to be bad news. And I did. Maybe I've found my place. I should be here and I want to be here."

"You're my brother. I can't leave you."

He squeezed her shoulders. The feeling was gentler this time. "You're my sister and you have to leave me.

Twenty-eight-year-old men shouldn't need their sisters to clean up their messes. They shouldn't need their sisters to hold their hands. They certainly shouldn't need their sisters to be there for them when they wake in the night screaming from a bad dream. You have to go, Si. Please."

Simone tried to speak, but she couldn't find any words to say. Dark images replayed through her mind. Not as intense, but memories she wouldn't be allowed to shake. What her life would be if she stayed within these walls. How she'd lose her brother and then herself.

In the distance was the echo of a trilling female voice, an exaggerated seductive call. Whoever she was, she was crying out for Robin. No, whoever they were, *they* were both desperate for him. Simone knew her brother could hear it too and wondered how long he could convince himself any of the solace he took in that direction was real. But then, maybe it was the numbness he wanted.

He'd be looked after here. She wouldn't be. Not in any way she'd want.

The house had won.

"I'll come back," she said, speaking quickly the words tumbled together. "I'll help you, I'll get you out of here."

"No. I'll come to you." He stated firmly. "I'm the one who found Breakspear, I brought us to him. Even that man on the street," his voice nearly cracked, but he held it together, "he was my responsibility. I did all of this and that means I have to take the lead in undoing it all. Not you. Me."

She shook her head, the tears returning. The last time they'd been apart was when she'd studied in

France. A lifetime ago.

"I can't believe you're saying goodbye to me."

He let go of her. "It's time, Si. Beyond time. And it's not goodbye. One day you'll look around and I'll be there. I promise you. I'll appear behind you and you'll hug me and it will be fantastic. But for now, we have to take separate paths."

"*Do you really believe you can possibly escape this?*" she wanted to ask.

But instead, from somewhere near came a squeal of both lust and impatience. Women's voices becoming louder and more ardent.

To her, they were the shrilling of Sirens. Robin probably thought so too, but he had convinced himself they were all he deserved.

She couldn't stay within those walls, she knew that. The house wanted rid of her and would torture her in any way it could. Make each moment excruciating until she ran. Now it was Robin's house, he couldn't leave. Not easily, not without Murkiss in tow and needing to come back soon.

Their separation was inevitable. Still, it felt overwhelming as she slowly stepped away.

Robin nodded to her once in sympathy. Him being the strong one for a change. She wondered how long he had before the deadness of this place infected him as it had Breakspear. Knowing she could do nothing to stop it.

A chasm opened between them in the hallway. He regressed to the boy with the cheeky smile he had once been. Playing cowboys with her in their garden, her always insisting she had the cap gun with the loudest bangs. She pictured them having dinner with her parents, the time they'd had as a family before disease took their father and then swiftly their mother. Dad could be playful and would try to reward them for eating everything on their plates by singing Elvis Presley songs to them. He was a terrible singer, but it made them laugh – made her laugh – and when they were young it was a great incentive. It always embarrassed Mum though, and because Robin took most after her, the embarrassment rubbed off on him too. Way before Simone was tired of it, Robin thwarted Dad's plans. Insisting he'd only eat the food on his plate if Dad *didn't* sing. Mum winking at him behind Dad's back as he precociously announced his new terms. It hurt Dad a little, but Robin wasn't able to see that. The two men in Simone's life never found a way to be on quite the same page as each other. She remembered holding Robin at their father's and then mother's funerals. The shock that, after Dad suffered for months, Mum went so quickly. "Busted like a fucking faulty lightbulb," as their uncle put it. She thought of the horror of the crash and how broken Robin had been for months afterwards. Then the idiosyncratic way he had put his life back together, and the fact she had followed him. Simone was always supposed to be the strong one, the one in charge, yet she allowed him to choose their path. After they started, she barely raised a qualm about the direction he was taking them. It hadn't really seemed *that* illegal, after all. Frankly, she was glad to see Robin alive. She loved to hear his laughter and his stories. And there was a lot of laughter and wild stories. There were many good times and companionship as they travelled the world. The people they targeted deserved to be hit in the wallets. And if the two of them lived a pleasant life while they did it, what was wrong with that? For nearly ten years, they had been more than a brother and sister, they had been an exceptional team, a partnership.

Now it was over.

Her feet, almost unbidden, had taken her half a dozen steps from him.

She looked over her shoulder at Robin, but neither said another word.

Simone had the absurd fear that when she reached it, the front door wouldn't open. The house would take perverse amusement in trapping her.

But of course it opened.

It felt as if the house flung her into the daylight. The sun was shining and the birds were singing far in the distance. She could almost believe she was waking from a terrible dream. If it wasn't for the sound of the door crashing shut behind her and the knowledge Robin was trapped within the walls of Breakspear Hall.

Feeling an ache in her chest, Simone took a deep breath, which was half a sigh and half a gasp.

Then she was struck hard in the side of the head.

CHAPTER THIRTY-FOUR

Simone fell sideways onto the driveway, scraping her palms against broken asphalt. With a scream, she shielded her head in her arms while simultaneously staring upwards. Not sure what she was expecting, unable to comprehend what last trick this house was playing on her.

It wasn't the house.

Instead, looming above her, was the short, ugly man from outside the casino.

His skin was pale and sweaty, but the sheer hatred in his eyes glowed. He'd punched her with his right hand, which now pointedly rested on the hilt of a knife protruding from his waistband. However, his gloved left hand hung free, blood dripping from the fingers so it resembled a cow's teat.

The snarl on his face was jagged and angry.

"No messing anymore, you cunt! I've no more fucking patience with you. *I want my money!*"

She scrabbled to her feet, expecting him to grab at her, but he wasn't quick enough. Shambling, he came forward, but to her it was like watching a Mummy from a black and white horror film. Simone was up in a half crouch before she answered him: "My brother has it!"

"What?"

"Not all of it. Some of it. This is our uncle's place and there's money in the safe. A hundred thousand pounds should you want it. All in cash."

She could see his face ponder. Pleasure and relief reflected in this new knowledge. His fingers still curled menacingly around the knife hilt.

"You better not be lying to me!"

"He's in the house! He can give you your money." She pushed herself swiftly but cautiously to stand. Knowing, at a head height taller than this man, he would not knock her down again without the element of surprise. "Go and see him!"

"Don't worry, I'll do that. I've had enough of him too. But I think I'll take a little collateral."

He lunged at her, tried to grab her bare arm. What he was intending to do, she wasn't sure. His left hand was obviously useless and he couldn't hold her and threaten her with his knife at the same time. It was academic though; he was too lead-footed in his movements. She easily eluded him, twisting the other direction.

Her eyes darted around and she saw the only car near the house was the old Silver Ghost Rolls-Royce. It meant he must have come up on foot. Simone turned and ran. There was no way he could chase her without a vehicle. She only realised later she didn't so much as glance back at Breakspear Hall. Her brother's new home.

Montagu Breakspear had told her the story of the burglar. He'd said the house would look after its owner, and she believed him.

Tears stained to her cheeks, she kept running.

CHAPTER THIRTY-FIVE

Maintaining a discreet distance, Jasper Redditch had followed them from the casino. Of course he had. They had his damn money and time was ticking against him. Every miniscule movement of his left hand screamed at him with how appalling his injury was. He couldn't let them get away.

It had been unfortunate about the old man. He felt bad about it. But then that's what happened when you crept up on someone with a knife, when you interrupted a man on a mission. What happened to him was hardly Jasper's fault. Not really.

And let's be honest, people would be sad for that old man in a way they never were for Jasper. Right then, Jasper was suffering. He was in pain and deserved sympathy. Something he knew from life's experience scarcely ever came his way. It was so unfair.

The wound where his finger used to be hadn't stopped bleeding, and he didn't have enough bandages with him to stem the flow. He felt weak and sick. There were moments when he had to concentrate to not feel dizzy, to not sail his car off the road into a lamppost. Honestly, he should have gone home, treated it properly, had a nap, refreshed himself. But the awkward truth remained: Sariah's body was bound to have been discovered and it wouldn't be long before Belinda's was too. He had to keep moving. He had to get his damn money.

So he drove across the city into South East London, not far actually – as a crow would travel it – from his own little place in Woolwich. But really a world apart. The surrounding homes weren't new-build, they were big Victorian piles. Those which hadn't been split into flats (and a flat around there would cost a fortune), were occupied by bankers and lawyers and other similar wankers. Not the sort then who would appreciate what it was to be a man with actual financial problems.

He only let himself stop when the Rolls-Royce ahead turned onto a little private driveway.

There was the temptation to roar in there and confront them. But he had no idea how many people might be on the property. It could be trouble if he charged in blindly. So, even though he had to listen to his own blood drip slowly onto the floor of his car and then pool beneath his feet, he knew he had to bide his time.

Sat behind the steering wheel, he waited. Uncomfortably aware if he didn't act soon, he'd pass out. Eventually he reached a compromise with himself whereby he left the car and walked up the private road. It was hard work. His head was light, and the bile was churning in the stomach; his left hand felt both heavy and as if it wasn't part of him at all. God, he could get gangrene! If he didn't get it treated soon, he feared he'd have to have it amputated at the damn wrist. (And the thought went through his mind of Sariah's mocking laughter from her place in Hell at him with one hand.) He did his best to stay vigilant. Ready to leap into the bushes at the sign of any activity ahead. Unless of course it was the thieving bitch or her brother. For them he carried the knife.

It took a long time. Unfeasibly long. Fucking dawn had broken and he'd foregone all notions of stealth. Now, not even bothering to hide well, he stood behind the nearest big tree to the house. Ready to pounce at his first opportunity. Hoping when the front door opened it wouldn't be a burly bloke.

His luck was in. It was the bitch sister. She'd been crying, her make-up was smeared and she clearly wasn't paying attention to where she was going or what was around her. The tart was easy enough to jump.

Unfortunately, she wasn't easy enough to keep hold of. There was no way he could catch her when she turned heel and ran. But at least she'd given him something. The brother was obviously behind it all. He was the one who'd connived the scheme, who'd flattered Belinda and got the old trout to sign those cheques. (Had he been so depraved a criminal he'd actually worked his way into her knickers too? Vomit rose to his throat. Certain gross things were barely worth contemplating.) It was the brother then who would make amends. He would hand Jasper the fucking money.

Steeling himself, pulling the knife free and clutching it tight in his good hand, he walked to the big house and – making as little sound as possible – pushed at the door.

It was unlocked.

The old and heavy hinges didn't even creak as he inched it open. Luck genuinely was on his side.

On entering, the first thing to hit him was the smell. Not damp and mould, but dead animal stench. Rats had evidently been allowed to crawl behind the walls and die. The room was vast. It should have been grand and impressive, but the brickwork was old and crumbling. They'd been left to ruin. What the hell was wrong with people that they'd let a great old house go to waste? It was outright disgraceful. He knew how to look after what he had. He wouldn't have squandered a property like this.

He shook his head. Some people were as fancy as la-di-dah, but really just scum.

There was no one visible as he crept forward, hoping not to tread on a creaky floorboard. There were numerous doorways branching off the hallway, as well as an impressively wide – predictably rotting – staircase.

Where the hell was the little shit?

Jasper nearly called out, before stopping himself with a muttered curse. It was the pain in his hand and his overall weariness which led to these rash impulses. He had to be circumspect.

Tossing a mental coin, tails decided him to try upstairs first. It was early morning and that wastrel struck Jasper as someone who'd enjoy a leisurely lie in. He'd probably only just gone to bed, in fact.

Jasper placed one foot on the stairs, when movement caught the corner of his eye from the other end of the hall. Someone appearing in a doorway and then ducking back. A person with a guilty conscience, perhaps. Hoping they weren't noticed.

Well, they were.

Now I have you, he thought.

He stepped off the stairs and gripped the hilt of the knife tight. The brother had been young and fit, so best to stab him straight in the guts and then make him crawl on his belly to his safe with the money.

Moving cautiously, Jasper stepped around the newel post. Whoever it was hid in the shadows. He'd convinced himself it was the brother, but as he trod closer, he realised it was a female rather than a male.

No matter, she'd be able to tell him where his prey was. And when he found the slimy bastard, he could use her as leverage.

But then, apparently finding confidence, this woman stepped towards him. And as he saw her, he nearly let the knife clatter onto the floor.

It was Belinda. At first he didn't recognise her. But as she stepped near, her badly broken face mended itself. Smashed bones and pulped cartilage healing; her skin renewing; the unbearably smug expression forming once again on her face. That dismissive look he thought he'd destroyed forever.

Jasper staggered bandy-legged, his left foot snagging on something on the floor, dropping him to his arse. Jarring his damaged hand as he did.

"No!" he cried. "*You* can't be here!"

For the first time in his life, he gave an almost feminine scream as another figure emerged from behind her shoulder. It was Sariah.

Unable to rouse his limbs from the floor, he watched helplessly as the two of them advanced on him.

"You can't be here!" he cried. "This isn't real!"

"We can do whatever we want!" Belinda told him, hateful superiority smeared all across her face. "You're far too pathetic to stop us."

Sariah smirked at her. "He always was an embarrassment to us, wasn't he?"

"Contemptible," agreed Belinda.

The two of them combined shoulder to shoulder. Becoming one. Big grins on their faces. Rictus and full of dark joy at what was about to happen. Those bitches were going to hurt him.

Desperately he tried to scramble away. Not caring if he dropped the knife, or about the pain in his left hand. All thoughts of even the money deserted him. His only concern was to get through the front door and run free down the driveway, much as that cow sister had done.

But he couldn't get to his feet.

He was half up on his knees when one cold, bony hand clamped unyielding around his left ankle. Then his right foot was seized.

The thing that was Sariah and Belinda yanked him upside down, pulled him into the air. The fingers of his good hand scraped at the floor for purchase, but he knew it wouldn't do any good.

Swaying, blood rushing to his head and his eyes bulging, the faces of his closest family filled Jasper Redditch's vision. They made him shriek uncontrollably.

The sounds of his prolonged, tortured death only slightly disturbed the new tranquil peace of Breakspear Hall. Only a few dozen feet away, for all the hours it lasted, the young master was too numb to notice.

CHAPTER THIRTY-SIX

Once she was free from the psychotic, bald man, Simone ran until the echo of her heartbeat boomed around her ears. She passed an old rusted car parked right at the end of the driveway which might have been the ugly man's. As she passed it she eyed it nervously. In case, although it was an unlikely scenario, he had a friend waiting. Even when Simone was on the road, she didn't stop running. Only stopping when, breathless, she reached a small high street and found the cafes selling morning coffees and the shops getting ready to open. Then, Breakspear Hall finally felt a safe distance from her.

It took her ten minutes to get a cab and then she headed straight to Park Lane and the hotel. Once there she instructed the driver to wait. Then she packed her things into her small suitcase and retrieved her passport. It hurt her to leave Robin's possessions behind, but to pack them all away as if he'd died would have been painful too. She had to get out of there. Her legs may have stopped moving, but she wasn't done running.

She told the cabbie to make one extra stop. Giving him the address for Lizzie's flat. It was a weekday, so she knew Lizzie would have already left for school, but she gave herself five minutes to feel sadness; even guilt. Lizzie had been suspicious that Simone would disappear from her life as quickly as she'd arrived. Probably not feeling as confident of the fact as she should have, Simone had reassured her she wouldn't. But here she was proving Lizzie right. Vanishing one morning without a word.

Of course, she knew Lizzie would open her arms and offer her comfort. But what would Simone say? How could she explain what she'd been through? Was there any way she could do it without contaminating Lizzie? Simone was too terrified to find out.

A portly cockney, who probably wasn't as middle-aged as his gut suggested, the cabbie asked more than once what they were doing there. Joking that if she was casing the joint, he didn't want to be an accomplice. She ignored him as much as she could and, after three hundred quick seconds had elapsed, told him to take her to Heathrow.

On the way, she wished she'd taken a shower. Yesterday morning was the last time she'd washed and she had got so dirty since then. Back at the hotel, she'd changed her dress for blue jeans and loose white top; then put the green dress – blood stains and all – into the bin. (Fortunately, the cabbie hadn't asked her what the stains were when he picked her up.) Now she wished she'd indulged an extra quarter of an hour to get clean. There was Breakspear's blood, obviously; but what of the blood which had run down the walls? Had any of it touched her? Had it dripped onto her hair, or landed on her skin? The cabbie didn't seem to notice if it had. He chatted the whole way out of London, a vague hint of flirtation beneath everything he said.

Desperately she tried not to think of Robin. If she tried to imagine what he was doing, or how he was feeling, she knew she would go insane.

They'd been together their entire lives. Even the brief time they'd spent apart, they had been in touch by text every day. When was she going to hear from him again?

Letting the cockney banter slip past her, she cracked open the window and watched the motorway going by. Her stomach was empty, but she also felt she might be sick. The shock and emotion of the last twenty-four hours pummelling into her. Her eyes stayed open, but her head lolled back on the seat. She lifted her face to the gap in the window, so she could take deep breaths of the gritty air blowing past.

She didn't know when it happened, but eventually the cabbie stopped speaking to her.

At the airport, she gave him most of the notes in her purse and then dashed into Terminal Three without properly thanking him or him properly thanking her. Once inside the building, she hurried to the nearest toilets. There she examined herself in the mirror. Her eyes were bloodshot, there were smears of make-up on her cheeks, and her hair needed both a wash and a brush. There were dark bags under her eyes and the worry lines on her forehead looked like they might sink into proper wrinkles and age her ten years. But she couldn't find any specks of blood anywhere. Not on her arms, not on her hands, not on her face, not in her hair.

Slightly more confident – or maybe it was her

weariness taking a different form – she walked back into the terminal with her credit card in hand.

The soonest flight leaving which had any seats available was one in two hours' time to Munich. A city she'd visited on a couple of occasions and always enjoyed. She purchased a single ticket. No return. It meant she was giving up on Robin, but to stay in the same city as him and know she couldn't reach him would have been unbearable.

There were two hours to kill before departure. She checked in her case, then made her way through security. Not quailing at all as the woman scanning her handbag regarded her suspiciously. She couldn't possibly know all Simone had been through. No matter how much her gaze pretended it did. Then Simone and her handbag took themselves to the first bar she spotted, where she bought two double vodkas. Medicine to stop her hands shaking.

Sat there, she thought about sex.

It was animalistic and ridiculous of her, she knew it, but she craved someone's hands on her. A physical sensation to take her out of herself. Drink would only do so much and, having gone through airport security, she wasn't able to buy hard drugs. But if she didn't do something, she would continue hearing the screams from Breakspear Hall. To see the blood running from the walls and feel the building closing in on her. Once again she'd have Montagu Breakspear's corpse lying by her side, and she'd be too fucking shell-shocked to let out a whimper. Here and now, she needed to feel pure naked pleasure. If she burst into hysterical tears straight afterwards, so be it, but she wanted another person's touch.

Alone in the bar, she checked out every woman who

went past. Even old ladies and mums walking by with their husbands and kids. Such was the darkness of her mood, she tried to convince herself men were attractive for the first time since she was a teenager. There were couples she gave the once over to. Determinedly, she tried not to think of Robin. Did her best not to picture him trapped between the walls of Breakspear Hall. A third and then a fourth vodka in front of her, she tried to fill her mind with good looking faces and toned bodies. When none were about, she imagined getting off with unsightly, fat bodies. Hair in the wrong places, cheap tattoos. Not caring about beauty. As long as whoever it was had working parts and knew what she (or even he) was doing, then she'd be close to happy. Shift her mind of what had happened, make her forget for (literally) five fucking minutes.

It was a dangerous mood in which she found herself, and Lord knows what would have happened if she hadn't met Helga.

No one approached her as she drank alone, and where would she have taken them if they had? A quick screw in the disabled toilet? That would pile griminess onto grimness. Besides, the time had ticked past faster than she thought it would. From now on she'd imagine each minute would be a lifetime of regret and worry, but vodka helped to quicken things a little. Not that she felt drunk. When her plane was called the second time for boarding, she pushed herself to her feet and caught her reflexion. In the dark light of the bar, she looked pretty damn good. Cool and confident, not sloppy or sozzled at all.

Her intention was to take her seat on the plane, then order a couple of little bottles. Keep ordering until the stewardess turned off the supply. Instead, she met a beautiful lady who was actually – and obviously – good for her.

The two of them sat next to each other. The only two people in a row of three seats. Helga was as tall as Simone, but lean and spare. A runner's body, the kind of woman who could complete a marathon before brunch and be so pristine she wouldn't need to shower afterwards. She had short, spiky auburn hair and features which were angular, but undeniably pretty. Especially when she smiled. Her entire face filled when she smiled, radiant and mischievous in equal measure. She had the most delightful accent: German, but with an Eastern European inflexion which reflected her Czech parentage. Her birthplace was Prague, but she had lived in Munich since she was three. She had studied there, made her home there, and these days worked as a doctor in the city.

"You look as though you could do with a friend," was the first thing she said to Simone. (In perfect English, which was great as Simone's German was beyond rusty.) It was an impeccably judged opener. Right from the beginning, Helga had a keen sense for what Simone needed.

They talked the entire journey, the attraction between them instantaneous. Helga had been at a conference, but mentioned in passing an ex-girlfriend who now lived in London, Simone responded by saying she and her last girlfriend had just broken up. Not mentioning it was that morning and Lizzie hadn't yet been informed. Was never going to be informed.

Helga made her feel better about herself. The darkness could have sunk deep into Simone, but being with Helga elevated her spirits. She was more than someone pretty to look at. Simone liked her, admired her. This young and charming doctor was conscientious and dutiful, qualities Simone could have done with more of in her life. She was also compassionate. Right from her first remark, Helga could see there was something wrong, but didn't pry. Let Simone know she was there and they could talk about it if she wanted. But if she didn't, that was fine too.

By the end of the flight, they were holding hands.

"Let's go for drinks!" suggested Helga when they landed. "You and I. I know a particularly attractive tucked away bar. And afterwards..."

"Afterwards?" asked Simone

"Well, what are your plans? Are you staying with friends? Checking into a hotel? Is there somewhere else you need to be? An appointment which means we can only have two drinks as opposed to five or six?"

Plans? Simone hadn't boarded the plane with anything resembling a plan. She was running.

"I know people in Munich. Sort of. I think I have their numbers in my phone. They might offer me a bed, if they're feeling in a generous mood."

"Well, that's it then!" Helga announced, waving her finger to brook no argument. "We'll go for drinks, we'll see if we're friends away from the recycled air of the aeroplane. And if we are, you can come and stay at my place. I have a spare bedroom, so there's no pressure or expectation. Though there might," she winked, "be a fair bit of hope."

Quite what she would have done in her sombre mood if she hadn't met Helga, she had no idea. Got off the plane with someone else, perhaps. Almost certainly she'd have found herself in a desperate situation. Instead, she let Helga lead the way through Arrivals. A taxi ride, two shots of schnapps each and a short walk later, they were at Helga's apartment. Of course, the spare bedroom remained unused. Its door not opened. They spent the night making love, their bodies excitedly entwined. Given how long it was since Simone had had any sleep, she should have collapsed. But closing her eyes onto darkness was nowhere near as much fun as this gorgeous lady she was with. It seemed as long as the two of them stayed together, neither of them would need any sleep and they wouldn't miss it.

In the morning, Helga had to kiss her goodbye. She looked especially fresh (and sexy as hell in the black trouser suit she was wearing for a meeting at her hospital), and in her polite – but pointed – way made it clear she wasn't kicking Simone out. This wasn't a one-night stand as far as she was concerned. She offered to buy Simone dinner that evening, and Simone said yes. The temptation to run faded. For now, she had gone far enough.

When she finally slept that day, it was dreamless. She had expected visions of Breakspear Hall, of Robin's face in agonies. But there was only blackness. On waking, the air tasted cool and clean. The sounds outside the window were a refreshing variety and she gazed at a picturesque Munich street. London was a thousand miles distant and felt a thousand years ago. As long as she could keep telling herself it was the case, she thought she might be okay.

What followed were three weeks of bliss. Unexpected and undeserved, but welcome. Whenever Helga wasn't working – and she swapped around as many shifts as she could to make the most of this new romance – they spent it together. It was as if they'd known each other years. More than once, Helga told her she was the best thing to happen to her in a long time. Could they be falling in love? Had Simone found her soulmate? If so, it was about bloody time. And just when it was most needed.

Whenever Simone had visited Munich previously, she had mainly hit the tourist haunts. Now Helga showed her the more off-the-trail cute neighbourhoods. Bars which were for locals and the better for it. They went to a museum or two hidden practically at the index of the guidebooks, Simone had had no idea they'd existed. The two of them held hands and felt no self-consciousness. Making each other laugh constantly, whispering sweet nothings and sharing looks private to them. And between the sheets, they were so compatible. Most nights they were intimate, Simone taking joy in Helga's quiet passion. In the playful seriousness with which she made love.

Things then should have been perfect for Simone, but of course they weren't.

Firstly, there were Simone's nightmares. That first day had been dreamless, but no night afterwards was. Once she woke screaming from the bottom of her lungs, a panicked Helga clutching her in the dark and trying to soothe her. It became an issue between the two of them. The first crack, but one which would grow into a chasm if nothing was done about it.

From the start, Helga was aware there was something amiss with Simone. On the plane, her offer to talk about it was easily rebuffed. They hadn't known each other, after all. Helga – so full of love and affection – thought that since they were now effectively living together, Simone should tell her all which worried her. No matter what it was, she would be there for Simone. She promised it to her with a kiss on the lips, and Simone knew she meant it completely.

But how could she talk of what had happened? How could she tell her about Breakspear Hall and the things she'd seen within it? There was no way, without breaking apart, she could discuss the trap her brother had made for himself.

So far, she had barely mentioned Robin to Helga. At the start, when they talked about families, she explained she was an orphan but she had a brother – although the two of them weren't close. Actually said those words, with a casual shrug, like they were nothing. Helga apparently saw her family frequently. She was lucky as they'd always been supportive of her.

Simone couldn't stop seeing Robin's face, though. Or Breakspear's blood on his clothes. Or how anguished he had been when they'd found him in the hallway. Or the stupid determination on his face as he took possession of Breakspear Hall.

It should have been her. She could have stayed, coped with it. Instead, she had turned coward and run. Abandoned her little brother.

"Whenever you feel ready for it." Helga stroked her cheek. She knelt in front of Simone, stunning in the early dawn light. Far too beautiful for any woman who had been rudely awoken. "I'm here for you, you know that, don't you? I am always here for you. And whenever you want to talk about it, you can trust me."

Whenever seemed way off in the future, but Simone knew it would have to be a sooner date.

All of her dreams had screams, and sometimes they bled into reality. She'd flinch at the imagined blood cascading relentlessly down the walls of Helga's fashionable Munich apartment. Over their time together, Helga repeated the same sentiment. Gently making a plea for openness. Each time, Simone nodded in understanding. Letting this kind and wonderful woman believe she was working her way to the moment of honesty. That eventually she'd open her mouth and all would come forth. Then they'd hug and cry together and nothing would feel as bad as it had once seemed.

If only this path was possible.

The second thing to impede this blossoming relationship proved far more fatal. The happier Simone became – and she knew deep inside, if she let herself, she could be happy with Helga forever – the more her soul rebelled. She knew it was wrong to be happy. Helga was all she'd ever wanted in a girlfriend, but there was too much self-hatred in her now to truly clutch on. Back in London her brother was suffering, she was sure of it, so how could she possibly waltz around Munich and pretend all was well? She couldn't comprehend a life where she enjoyed herself anymore. There was no way she deserved happiness. It didn't matter if it was open to her.

Maybe, towards the end of the wondrous twenty-one days they spent together, Helga sensed her drawing away. If that was the case, she was subtle in her attempts to keep hold of Simone. There was no sulking, nor screaming arguments. Instead, more and more, Helga held her and stroked her hair and let Simone know she was there for her if she would simply let her in. Neither of them mentioned 'love'. As intense as their relationship was, they were both conscious of how short a time they'd known each other. So neither of them said it out loud, but it definitely hung between them.

Unfortunately, love was something Simone didn't deserve.

That night three weeks in, when Helga was on a late shift, Simone went to a lesbian bar the two of them had danced in twice. It was no impulsive decision. Mid-afternoon, she'd gone to a boutique and bought herself a cute and sexy red dress. When she left Helga's apartment, her hair was primped and her lips were scarlet.

She planned to do something stupid that night. Her recklessness was with forethought.

Back at Heathrow, she'd felt bereft of control and been lucky enough to meet Helga. However, she didn't deserve this good fortune, so she went out and met Veronique.

Apparently Veronique was an actress. She made sure Simone knew this within the first three and a half minutes of chatting, then kept mentioning it the rest of the evening. Undoubtedly she was gorgeous enough to be an actress. When Simone saw photos of her later in the French swords and sorcery series in which she starred, she was impressed. Veronique spent her entire time on screen clad in a tight black leather top, which crossed over her cantilevered breasts, and a skirt which was slit to the top of both her thighs. An outfit which did an outstanding job of showing off – over-showing even – the fabulous voluptuousness of the young woman's body.

In physique, she was the exact opposite of Helga. Whereas Helga was long and lean, Veronique was short and almost exploding lubriciously. Ripe pretty much to the point of parody. She must have known herself that fat would eventually overtake her. One day she'd no longer be the young sexpot and, if she continued acting (although Simone had no idea how much 'acting' she did in that outfit), it would be as a chubby character actress. But at least she'd have thousands of photos and hundreds of hours of film footage to look at and see how gorgeous she had been.

Her personality too was a lot different to the young German doctor's. It was there in her conversation, right from the beginning, how thoroughly absorbed she was in herself.

"Chérie," she would say at the start of every sentence. Veronique didn't speak English, but fortunately Simone's French was extremely good. "I couldn't possibly play dowdy or bedraggled. I am a beautiful lady and the audience wants to see me as a beautiful lady. They do not want me with mud splattered on my face. Maybe across my tits, yes. I imagine quite a few would want to see that. But it isn't the kind of show we're making, thankfully. But no mud over my face. They want to see it pristine, because it is pristine."

She did pay attention to Simone, told her how attractive she was. Pretty enough to become an actress, even. But it was obvious to Simone that she was only playing nice because she wanted to sleep with her. Veronique was prepared to ask a few questions and go through the necessary, but really she was there to talk about herself and for Simone to stare at her admiringly. It was Simone's role to adore the fact she could ever have a brief sliver of Veronique's time, let alone become her lover. There was never an instant when Simone was fooled by her, but she went along with it anyway. The woman was selfish, impulsive and capricious. An obvious bitch. But Simone had arrived wanting to do something idiotic and Veronique served.

In bed too, the differences with Helga were stark. Whereas Helga was a wonderful lover who channelled her passion into satisfying her partner; Veronique kissed sloppily and lay there, only really caring if she got off.

It was an obvious disaster, but since Simone couldn't let herself be happy, she ran willingly in its direction. They slept together and, in the morning, got a cab to Helga's apartment where Simone grabbed her passport and a few items of clothing and make-up. Filling her small case once again. Then the two of them flew to Paris. Drinking champagne at nine in the morning and giggling at their big, exciting, naughty adventure.

Much as with Lizzie, Simone did not say goodbye to Helga. She walked out on this woman who cared for her so much, who she knew she could be happy with, and threw what they had into the bin. No, more than that, she effectively took a shit on it along the way. At the time she didn't try to justify it, but nor did she feel ashamed of herself. It was something which had to happen, which she needed to do.

She knew shame and regret would come later. There'd be a long time to rue what she'd done. But she couldn't stay with Helga, just as she couldn't stay with Lizzie. Eventually both would have expected her to open up to them. And the fact she couldn't would have become a roadblock. Even before Breakspear Hall, she would have hated to confess everything about herself. Who wanted to admit they were a con artist who partly made an income pretending to be sexually interested in corrupt old men with money? After Breakspear Hall though, there was no way she could articulate all which was in her head. And with it looming constantly in her mind, she knew she couldn't fall in love and couldn't let herself be loved. It was much better to disappear.

With Veronique it was easy. This was only ever going to be a fling. The two of them would never stay together. She could get her thrills, such as they were, and move on.

Still, it fell apart much sooner than she expected.

In Paris they checked into a five-star hotel near the Arc de Triomphe and, within hours, the true situation became apparent. Veronique wasn't interested in a lover in the normal sense. Back home – a mere five minute drive from their hotel room – she had an older banker husband and a four-year-old daughter. It seemed to Simone that Veronique had been caught up in the thrill of their lesbian fling in Munich and, now she had brought her to Paris, was struggling to see how Simone would fit into her life. The only idea she could conjure – and a suggestion she voiced with actual earnest seriousness – was that Simone become a kind of au pair and threesome partner for her and her husband.

Despite the dark place in which she found herself, this was not a notion which appealed to Simone.

The two of them argued. Screaming at each other across the soft furnishings of the bedroom. Veronique believing Simone was indebted to her as she'd paid for the plane tickets, despite Simone offering her own credit card. When Simone didn't immediately back down, Veronique branded her an "ungrateful dyke slut!" Really Simone should have slapped her face; but instead she stopped her own yelling, picked up her small case and marched past a seething Veronique. The actress so red-faced and clenched it appeared she would go full Vesuvius. Walking down the hotel corridor, Simone knew she would never see that stupid woman again. But she also realised Helga would be arriving home about then and wondering where the hell she had gone. Would have a sinking, heart-breaking fear in her belly that Simone had indeed done the unthinkable.

Alone in Paris unexpectedly that afternoon, Simone toured bars. There was more vodka and, this time, she mixed it with a couple of pills she purchased from an overly muscular barman. He explained to her what they were all were, but she didn't listen. Just enjoyed the fuzziness she got off them.

By evening, she was in a basement dive in The Bastille. And there she allowed herself to be chatted up by a man.

When she was younger, a lot younger, she had a few dalliances with men. However, the only one she'd gone to bed with was this strikingly good looking surfer type. A ten out of ten, as an excitable straight friend had giddily told her. Even then, she found the experience highly disappointing.

The man she met in The Bastille was short, chubby and balding, with a goatee beard. The latter grown presumably to stop his bland face being impossible to remember five minutes after meeting the guy. If she'd been straight, she doubted she'd have fancied him. That night, however, well, his conversation kept her amused. He wasn't a narcissist, and was pretty witty. Not funny, but humorous. Besides, he was happy to buy her drinks and smile through her own wandering conversation. Too much booze and too many little yellow pills meant she couldn't focus too well. They had a fairly entertaining evening, or as entertaining as they could manage in a dive like the one they found themselves. And at the end of the night, when he placed his hand on her knee and asked if she wanted to accompany him to his hotel room, she said, "Okay."

She didn't explain she was gay or offer any other excuse. The thought of trying to find a hotel to check into herself bored her. It was better to agree and continue doing stupid things, as that meant she was at least doing something. Better to take her mind off Helga, off Lizzie, off Robin.

His room was boxy and small, a traveling salesman's cage, a world away from the luxurious suite in which Veronique had promised they could order cocktails and oysters. The walls had ugly, striped, patterned wallpaper; while the bedsheets were more grey than white. All the furniture was imitation chestnut. Through the open wardrobe door she could see cheap wire coat hangers. The only vague attempt at prettification was a rectangular painting of a beach, which would leave her even more depressed if she stared at it. It was a room to make the soul sad. But as she was there, she may as well make the best of it.

Sat in the bar, with him buying her drinks, she hadn't realised he only came up to her shoulder. Now in the hotel room, he pawed at her and nibbled her and – unmoving – she let it happen. She had been glancing around to see if there was a minibar, or at least a drinks menu they could call down from. But when he touched her, she froze. She didn't kiss him back, didn't reach out for him. Instead, simply stood there: a mannequin he had taken an erotic interest in. He was a long way from the beauty of Helga, or the prettiness of Lizzie (or the nasty sexiness of Veronique), but maybe this was what she deserved. A man with a round face, round shoulders, middle-aged spread, the slight smell of stale sweat and the impossible to credit belief he would be a wonderful lover to her.

He had taken his shirt off, revealing a hairy and grey chest, but she still wore her dress. The same one from the bar in Munich last night. With chubby paws he groped her and she let him. Not believing he would actually lay her on her sheets and make love to her, but willing – she supposed – to go along with it if he tried.

Except, when he pulled her skirt up and bent to slobber over her naked left thigh, she grabbed what hair was left on his head, yanked his face up and slapped him.

His cheek went red, both with the impression of her hand and from the sheer shock of it. He appeared understandably confused.

The situation was funny, she thought, and almost laughed out loud. To see his confidence evaporate, to see his face crimson and his torso clenched together was cruelly amusing. He didn't retreat though. This was clearly what she was into and so he would enjoy it too.

The bulge in his trousers was proof to it.

"Hit me!" she ordered, both woozy and breathless. She slapped him across the face again, harder, in case he didn't know what a 'hit' was.

Such was his ardour and his claimed virility, she thought he'd be instantly into it. That he'd want to hurt her. Show her who was boss. The beautiful woman he'd lured to his hotel room and not only fucked, but left bruises on. But no, this had gone a direction he wasn't anticipating and one he would have to work himself up to. Or maybe she would have to work him up. She clouted him even harder – the other cheek – her fingers and thumb leaving five beautiful lines. It was like pressing into clay.

Finally, he responded. Lifting his right hand and shaping to slap her. He hesitated, however, until she demanded – her voice furious – that he did it as fucking hard as he fucking could. His best wasn't much though, an enthusiastic pat rather than the blow she'd inflicted on him,

It was nothing. It didn't hurt.

Nevertheless, it broke something inside of her. She screamed. So loud and shrill, he jumped. Mouth open, eyes wide, hands spread to placate her, he leapt away from the bed. The bulge in his trousers looking more stupid than anything else. His jaw opened and shut, but he did not understand what to say, had no idea what to do. He wasn't sure what was happening.

"Please..." he muttered.

Although whatever the thought was, he didn't finish it.

She'd already espied the half full glass of water on the fake chestnut bedside table. With no consideration of consequences, she snatched it up and swung it at him. Rage and contempt boiling together, she roared as she did it.

In the small room, there was an explosion which rattled the sad picture of boats and sand. It all happened far too quickly. The glass shattered and then there was blood. Bright spurts of the stuff, shooting towards her and hitting the downward stripes on the walls like an unwelcome rain shower.

The man dropped to the floor without a murmur. His trouser bulge a deflating balloon.

Shrieking, she collapsed to the carpet too. Her hands reaching to his throat and trying to staunch the flow. It was hopeless. His eyes had less life in them by the second.

At some point, her screaming stopped and she sat on the floor with her arms wrapped around her knees. She rocked back and fore, trying to make sense of it. There was blood on the walls once more. Again there was a dead body lying next to her. It was as if she'd never left Breakspear Hall. It had accompanied her all this way.

She expected a knock on the door. Hotel security, or maybe the gendarmes, ready to take her into custody. She'd have gone with them happily.

But nobody came.

Surely someone must have heard her cries. Once they did, you'd have thought they'd have called the police. However, apparently no one was much alarmed. Perhaps this was the kind of hotel where the odd scream wasn't uncommon.

She didn't know over how long a period, but slowly she pulled herself together. Her mind turned to her brother. Imagining him covered in blood. Viscous red sheathing his skin and pouring from every orifice. Alone next to the stranger's corpse, she thought of how much she missed Robin, how she was wrong to have abandoned him.

Simone knew her brother wasn't dead. What he was going through was much worse.

Silent now, she considered the dead man beside her. Another reason she could never be happy again. Did he have a wife? A girlfriend? Who were his family? His friends? She'd never find out. But she had marked their lives forever.

Hours must have passed and no one came. Gradually she forced herself to move, making it to the toilet to puke. Then she stripped off her clothes and had a shower. A good half an hour she spent in there, making sure every millimetre of her face and body was clean. In her small case, she found the jeans and T-shirt she'd worn to flee London, and put them on. Once again she left a bloody dress in a hotel room bin.

She knew it was wrong, but she didn't look at the man as she left the room. What would be the point? She couldn't get any guiltier, or feel any worse. And she was the wrong person to utter any kind of eulogy. Instead she snuck out, pretending to be only a one-night stand. Or a hooker. Then she went unobtrusively through the lobby, walked up the street a hundred yards and hailed a cab to Charles de Gaulle Airport.

A friend of hers – well, a friend of Robin's really, but Simone had his number – had a guesthouse in the Hollywood Hills and, more than once, had said Simone could use it.

She was finally going to gracefully accept the offer, and then she would drink herself to death.

CHAPTER THIRTY-SEVEN

Maxwell was a hairdresser to celebrities who'd played around in the same circles as Robin, back when Robin was young, callow and loved to party. Gay himself, he had nevertheless been so entranced by Simone's locks he'd offered to always style them for free. An invitation she'd frequently taken up. The two had formed a sort of friendship, which lingered in a couple of text messages every six months kind of way, even after he moved to Los Angeles and styled the hair of Scarlett, Brie and the various Jennifers. He globetrotted a lot, but had his main house in the Hollywood Hills, with a second – bigger than many three bedroom semi-detached family homes in London – place on the same grounds. After a few exchanged messages in the back of the cab, the Hollywood Hills spare house was hers for the foreseeable.

It wasn't as glamorous as she'd pictured, but it was perfect. A big box of a building, with a king-sized bedroom, two unused doubles, an open-plan kitchen and living area, with an enormous bay window overlooking the hills. What made it better from her current perspective was that Maxwell himself wasn't in attendance. He was working in Morocco and had a new boyfriend in Santiago, and so was bouncing between those two locales. But he trusted her and was thrilled she'd finally taken him up on his kind offer. Before she arrived, he arranged for one of his flunkies to put a fruit basket, some Californian white wine and two truly expensive bottles of his branded shampoo in the lounge as a housewarming present.

So she settled into a city she didn't know in a house all by herself.

It suited her mood completely.

Her mobile phone was allowed to die. She shut the door on the outside world as best she could and spent six long months there – drinking, popping pills and smoking unhealthy quantities of weed. Putting on weight, becoming puffy around the cheeks and not caring in the slightest. She let each afternoon drift into evening, right through the night and into morning.

One day she realised that she had turned thirty a few weeks before. None of her friends had been able to reach her to congratulate her. If Robin had realised the date, he'd never have been able to get hold of her even if he wanted to. She toasted the non-event late and alone.

Despite what she'd done in the immediate aftermath in Europe, she didn't have sex. The drug dealer Maxwell had hooked her up with as part of the house propositioned her pretty much every time he saw her. Even as she let her hair hang greasy and did not try to hide her extra weight. He drooled over her with a lasciviousness which said less about the resilience of her natural beauty, and more about how unfussy he was.

Of course, no encouragement came his way. All their transactions took place on the doorstep. She feared if she let him in – so much as a crack – she would kill him. To let anyone over the threshold would be an invitation for the blood to flow down the walls.

And she was seeing enough of that already.

Both inside and outside the house, the walls had a fresh coat of bright white paint. They glimmered and shone in the Californian sunshine. However, she watched blood pour down them, saw it spray afresh across the brilliant gloss each day. From the corner of her eye, it would drip from the ceiling. Unceasingly. A wound which, once opened, could never be healed. All she had to do was look in their direction and the most pristine of walls became a splattering of gore.

In those strange breathless moments between her nightmares and the numbness she called waking, she could sense the viscous red gushing towards her. She'd wake and think blood was coating her, that it was thick and warm across her skin. All she had to do was open her mouth, she imagined, and it would spew between her lips and never stop, drowning her.

Hating to sleep, she nevertheless knew she couldn't stay awake forever. Roughly sixty-two hours was the longest she managed, but collapse into fevered dark dreams was inevitable.

She pictured the man in the hotel room in Paris. His startled expression when his throat slashed open. Blood once again spraying everywhere. She never saw them properly, but she dimly pictured crying friends and relatives. The grief of all those who knew and loved him.

Her thoughts of Helga and Lizzie were bittersweet.

They couldn't know it, but they'd both had a phenomenally lucky escape.

And then there was Robin. She thought of him most of all. Alone in Breakspear Hall, the blood running down the walls for him too.

She had run six thousand miles, but the blood had surged after her. There was no way to make it stop.

For that reason she couldn't invite anyone in. She couldn't open herself up. Her only hope was to try to alter her headspace and drink herself into oblivion.

But oblivion turned out not to be deep enough.

The realisation came to her, slowly, that her life could go one of two paths. She could continue fucking herself over, until one day – a couple of weeks after anyone last saw her – a team of paramedics would be called to her rigor-mortised body. Either it would be the drink and drugs, or it would be a knife. Often she stood in the kitchen and held out the sharpest blade. Considering cutting herself, fantasising about slicing at others – even though no other real person was about.

The path to destruction was calling her, and she could take it. Or she could go back.

Return to Breakspear Hall and try to liberate her brother. Stop him from enduring endless tortures every day.

For a good three months of her stay she told herself on first awaking, either in the day or night – her throat like a stained ashtray – that she had to book plane tickets. She had to get herself together and fly to London. But each time she reached for a bottle instead.

Blood still poured from the walls.

A ghostly echo of Breakspear Hall.

Robin calling for her.

Needing her help.

And she knew she had to go to him, just as she'd always done, but for the longest time she was too petrified to move. It was easier to get drunk and high, and hope on this occasion when she passed out, the screaming dreams wouldn't get her.

CHAPTER THIRTY-EIGHT

After a nine-hour flight, and fifty-one hours of painful sobriety, Simone finally returned to London. She arrived at Heathrow carrying only a handbag. Her suitcase left in a closet at Maxwell's place.

Maybe as a European, her horniness was keener on her home continent. Even in Brexit London. There was the great temptation, the second she arrived, to head to a Soho bar she knew and try to meet someone pretty. (Or not so pretty, she didn't really mind.) See if she retained the knack now she was plumper than she'd ever been. It would be great to stretch out on crisp hotel room sheets with a lady absolutely delicious. Then maybe they could go for breakfast, or eat breakfast off each other. They could hang out. She'd been born in Kent, but this was Simone's home city. There were a thousand different places she knew to go. Beautiful streets, quirky bars, chic cafés. They could get to know each other, maybe fall in love. Her actions had been too monstrous for her to seek out Lizzie (or Helga, for that matter), but maybe she would get a third bite. A girl could daydream, after all.

But no, she knew if she did, it would be a trap as tight as the one in which she'd snared herself in LA. It sounded fun, a taste of pleasure before the unpleasant job ahead, but she'd soon be getting drunk and high and trying to pull every night as a way to distract herself. Besides, if she fell in love, the same problem would remain. She could never tell the woman in question her truth. What she'd done in Paris, why she'd returned to London. Then there were her nightmares, the amount of times she shot awake screaming. How would she explain any of it?

No, any attachment would be a distraction. A wonderful distraction, to be sure, but one which would leave the poor woman hurt and Simone wretched. If it was possible for her to get any more wretched.

It was time to make things right.

She had come for Robin, to try to save her brother from the trap in which he found himself. One where the blood genuinely flowed down the walls and the nightmare visions of dead people weren't just dreams, they were his daily reality. Breakspear Hall would look after him, she knew that. It would try to anyway. But how long before his soul was no longer satisfied? How long before the house drained his spirit completely to get its own way? Or he wanted to leave and it terrified him into staying?

They'd met in the casino, but Robin had never talked privately to Montagu Breakspear. He hadn't seen, as she had, the defeat forever in his eyes. She couldn't imagine Breakspear (even when he was in a young man's body), ever looking hopeful. She wondered when was the last time Breakspear had optimistically expected anything in life. It was no doubt moments before he first walked through the doors of the house which bore his family name.

Six months of solitude and bad dreams meant her visions frequently entwined themselves with remembered reality. When she pictured old Breakspear's eyes, they were in Robin's head. It was her brother's lost and ruined gaze she saw.

Now she wore a black high-necked dress – a presentable garment ordered on ASOS. The colour seemed appropriate. It wasn't a funeral she was going to, but she felt funereal. Sitting in the back of an equally black cab, she gave the little silver-haired cabbie the address for Breakspear Hall, but asked him to make a stop along the way. She needed to buy supplies.

Traffic was surprisingly good, and the man was nowhere near as chatty as his counterpart who'd taken her to Heathrow. He only became effusive when he saw how big a tip she gave him. Simone had withdrawn two hundred and fifty pounds from a cash machine on arrival. The man might as well have all of it.

Then she stepped into a chilly Spring evening, looked around at a street she barely recognised, then turned and walked up the overgrown private driveway towards the big, gothic house. Each step felt like she was striding towards her own gravestone.

She shuddered when she saw it at the top of the hill. There it was, as black and imposing as in her most dreadful dreams. Its turrets somehow more twisted; the house – along with that vine squeezed around it – growing deformed and ugly out of the black soil. The sun was setting, but she noticed not a single window reflected any light. She was reminded obliquely of doll's eyes. Staring at a dozen of them all lined up together, no life within them at all.

In front of her loomed the enormous front door. Its big brass knocker refusing to gleam. The doorway was not in the slightest sense welcoming. It yelled at all visitors to keep the hell away, but her in particular. There was no need to erect a rude sign.

The house didn't want her there, but Simone had known that would be the case. However, Robin was within, doomed to spend the rest of his days between those walls, and somehow she had to save him.

That's what every vision of blood had brought her to. They may have been warning her to keep away – screaming across the Atlantic that returning was a bad idea – but instead they had drawn her to this moment.

Robin was her brother and it was her job to look after him. It had always been her job. He may have done a couple of awful things in his life, but never maliciously. He did not deserve this.

Swallowing her rising vomit, Simone straightened, clutched her handbag to her side and walked the final few steps to the front door. The building itself was a monster from a fairy tale.

CHAPTER THIRTY-NINE

Besides the front door was an old rusty doorbell. She hadn't noticed it the last time she was there, but there was no way it was new. Although, who could say anything for certain about Breakspear Hall? Taking a deep breath, she reached out her finger, which she willed not to tremble.

The bell was mechanical. It clanged once in the distance, an ominous dull thud which did not echo.

Peering at the front door, she felt a frightened little girl. Blood pounded in her head, sheer nerves and fear making her jangle. She wanted to quit and run, of course she did. But she knew if she gave way to cowardice, she'd eventually have to turn around and come back to this door. It would be much harder the second time.

She clutched her handbag tighter in her hand. This had to be done.

There was no sound from within at first. It was inconceivable anyone at home could have missed the clang of the bell, but nothing happened. This time it was going to be impossible to keep her digit from shaking as she reached again for the button.

Then suddenly, the door opened. Once more without a creak. It swung onto the darkness inside and before her – bland face smiling curiously – was Murkiss.

His butler's uniform was immaculate, as always. While his face was outwardly as round and harmless as it had first appeared. She knew better than to be fooled. She saw what was really in his eyes, a brutal hatred. A desire not to welcome, but to destroy.

"Miss Simone," he purred, the disapproval gentle in his tones. "What a pleasant surprise."

He in no way meant it. Was he even surprised? Had he known she was coming? If he had, wouldn't the house have done more to stop her?

"I want to see my brother." Her tone was implacable.

"Of course." He gave a deferential nod of the head. However, there was a hesitation before he moved, a calculation. Maybe wondering whether to simply slam the door in her face. He didn't. Something must have returned her to the horrors of Breakspear Hall, and curiosity as to what it was got the better of him. "Please come in," he said finally.

Murkiss stepped to one side, opening the vast expanse of darkness behind his shoulder. A challenge to her. Seeing whether she'd have the guts to walk in willingly now she knew what lay within.

Despite her insides screaming, she did not quail.

It was impossible to tell if he was grudgingly impressed as he watched her step over the threshold. Without a word, he shut the door behind them.

Once inside the hallway, she could see a little more.

But the large space had an oddly inchoate quality. As if it hadn't been finished. She could tell it wasn't the elegant sight which had greeted her and Robin when they'd first entered all those months ago. Nor was it the crumbling ruin which threw her out. It was tidy, but austere. Maybe, since it was Robin's place these days, this made a certain sense. The last time he'd properly had a home he'd been a teenager, most of his life had been in hotels. He thus had no interest in home furnishings.

The butler waved his arm in a sweep, pointing her in the direction of the second doorway beyond the stairs, testing again whether she had the courage to step forward. She did. The two of them falling into step beside each other.

"And how was your trip?" Murkiss asked.

"Trip?" She asked dumbly, but knew instantly it answered a question dark in her mind. This house had known where she was the entire time.

"You have been abroad, haven't you?" asked Murkiss, conversationally. "I understand you have been to a great many places I should wish to visit. The Continent. America, as well. Such an exciting itinerary. But then, perhaps I am easily impressed. I have never really travelled, there's always been too much to do here."

There was a moistness to his voice. Even in his practised smoothness, the words sounded sticky. They were unctuous, oozing and dripping at the same time. A sound more chilling than charming. If he'd stared at her arms, he would have seen goosebumps rising. But then she knew it wasn't really a man's voice, it was the house speaking through him, its conduit.

Murkiss continued: "And such wonderful people

you met. Particularly your German friend. Tell me, have you heard from her recently?"

That floored her. His words then stopped her. Simone felt as though she'd been punched in the gut. She spun on her heels and his face, so innocent, made her feel sick. The darkness deep in his eyes was glowing. She was about to burst out with something angry, though she had no idea what, when the man seemed to melt into the air.

She realised behind his vague shape, through the open second doorway on the right, stood Robin. He was by the window, stark naked, his bare backside facing her. He was staring into the blinding light beyond, apparently seeking something.

The anger died in her throat as she uttered her brother's name. Not a friendly 'Rob', but a startled "Robin!" Spluttering, so it turned from two separate syllables into different words.

It was enough. His shoulders tensed and then he turned his head, gazing around slowly to see if she was really there. Not believing it.

For the first time in six months, she regarded the face of her brother in the flesh. His skin was so smooth, his hair piled in curls and his tan almost permanent. He appeared as he did when he was nineteen years old and had been so beautiful and full of promise. Before the bad dreams, before the worry lines had a chance to develop around his eyes, before the heavy anxiety he did his utmost to hide. Once again he was the handsome boy who could stride out and take the world.

Undoubtedly, she gasped as he turned his face towards her. Echoing his exclamation of surprise.

For a few seconds it was obvious that he couldn't

believe she was really there. He turned full to face her. Unabashed, not embarrassed by his nakedness. His expression caught between a full smile and confused shock. Hesitantly, as if not trusting she could be real, he took a step towards her.

And as he did, his beauty fell away. Unfathomable pain replacing it.

CHAPTER FORTY

"What are you doing here?" His voice was already choked by tears.

He'd appeared young, but his voice was old and weary. Cracked. His beauty had been an illusion and, up close, it wasn't hard to peer through the façade.

His feet stumbled. She tried to catch him, before he dropped to his knees on the floor. Instead, both of them crumpled, flopping together almost in slow motion. Robin ended up lying on his back across her lap, wrapped tight in her arms.

"What on earth are you doing here, darling?" he asked. "Why did you come, Si?"

"I had to. I couldn't leave you."

He gazed blank eyed at her. "But you had to go. I did this for you. One of us had to stay and it was better it was me. We agreed."

"You agreed," she chided him, gently.

"But you shouldn't be here, you shouldn't."

He buried his head in her breast and sobbed uncontrollably. Great moans of pain racked his body which was no longer toned and tanned, but grey and emaciated. She clutched tight around his torso, and with her left hand stroked through his hair. As luxuriant as it appeared, strands of it came loose in her fingers.

"Where's Murkiss?" he asked, tremulous with genuine fear. "It doesn't matter. He's always around. Always around."

"How has it been, darling?"

"It's…" She saw him struggling but he couldn't immediately find the right words.

She shushed him, running her fingers across his cheek. "It's okay, I'm here for you. I will look after you, as I always did."

"But you shouldn't be here!" he gasped. "I can handle this. I told you that. It's been hard, true. I thought I could lose myself in the women, but interest is swiftly sated when you know none of it is real. When there's no human being to form a connection with. But I've been thinking, I've been planning, I haven't been idle." He squeezed his anguished fingers around her arm. "Somehow I can find my way out, I know I can. I've got out of scrapes before."

She could have murmured he'd had a kind of luck on his side then, luck which had evidently deserted him, but those words would be unhelpful.

His voice went small. "How long has it been, Si? How long?"

"Six months," she said, with regret.

"Really?"

"Does it surprise you?"

It took half a minute for an answer to form on his lips. "I don't know. If you told me six days or six years, I think I would have felt the same."

"Breakspear was here for decades," she reminded him. A jail sentence, one which he couldn't have been deserved.

"I don't know how." Anguish creased him. "It's like living in a fantasy, Si. A cruel fantasy. I can do whatever I want, do *whoever* I want. They offered me you on one occasion."

The revulsion passed through them both. His eyes told her the offer had been angrily rejected.

"But none of it is real," he continued. "The problem with endless fantasy is you miss the things which are real. You miss having actual people to care for you. I haven't spoken to anyone who wasn't this house for… for… half a year. Half a fucking a year without a single word or touch or glance of genuine affection. Nothing is real, everything is empty."

She stroked his hair and let him weep a little more. Then, as softly as she could, she turned his face up so his attention was fixed solely on her.

"Darling," she said.

"Yes, darling." He mouthed the words.

"Can you call Murkiss for me, please? He was here a moment ago and I want to speak to him."

His bottom lip trembled.

"Please."

"I don't want to."

"I know." Her tone was all sympathy. "But I need you to. I have to speak to him. I have to talk to the house."

He swallowed, before acquiescing with a pained wince.

"Thank you." She kissed his sweaty forehead.

The reluctance never left his face, but then he squeezed his eyes shut.

Murkiss did not immediately appear. Instead, in less than a tick of the clock, a thousand faces burst from the walls, each one screaming at her.

CHAPTER FORTY-ONE

Sometimes she told herself those faces she'd seen bursting from the walls were dark imaginings, but she knew she was rationalising the experience to herself. (And had been incredibly glad when they hadn't emerged from the brilliant white walls in LA.) She had wanted the butler, as at least he appeared human, but after the first flinch she held herself steady. This was the house as well. It was just greeting her in exposed form.

The sound hit Simone and Robin first. Blasting from deep below. Hell itself, or a more terrible realm adjacent. The cries charged through the stagnant air; a wailing choir, a cacophony of suffering entwined with gleeful sadism. There were mocking sounds, pained sounds. Cries of the tortured and the torturers. The floorboards, the sparse furniture and walls all rattled to the point of destruction. Only the crescent window, and the overcast evening light beyond, held still. A bizarre fixed point to hold one's gaze on, to think about what life might be like outside. But another tool to excruciate, she realised. Outside seemed far away. As did sanity. A glimmer made the dread worse.

Her hair was blown back by the explosion of noise and the release of sour, stale air. In her arms, Robin shook. They trembled together.

Six months had passed and she imagined maybe he'd have got used to what Breakspear Hall could do. Perhaps though he'd done everything the house wanted and had never experienced it fully until now. More likely, it was impossible for one's mind to become used to these torments.

"Slut!" A thousand voices roared. "Whore! Wanton bitch! Rancid immoral cunt!"

Robin quaked against her. She thought he yelled something, asking it to "leave her alone", but his voice didn't impact the grating, horrific noise. She stayed still, did not let those voices ruffle her. Alone in the blood-stained walls of the Hollywood Hills, she had prepared herself for this and more.

"Foul unnatural harridan!" they roared.

She'd merely glimpsed them before, but now the faces burst fully from the walls. They were uniformly old, wrinkled and riddled with pestilence. Even the young amongst them – and tragically there were boys in their number – gave the impression of having endured millennia. Theirs were rotting visages. Skin grey, cheeks sunken, teeth missing. The only remote sign of life within them was their eyes glowing red. But it contained nothing of humanity.

Within this sea of pain and hatred, she found one face she recognised. Breakspear's. But he was older than he'd ever been before. The intense sadness had been scrubbed away, leaving twisted features which snarled with as much hatred as every other bastard.

The image of his dead body crumpled on the floor rose unbidden, as did the knowledge he'd died actually trying to help them.

Joining them only seconds later was the shape of Murkiss himself. At her side suddenly, hands behind him, but any pretence of deference gone. His shoulders were straight and his head was held high. The same red light glimmered in his eyes as it did in all those other ghoulish faces.

"How can we help you, Miss Simone?" His tone wasn't a fury filled scream, but the contempt scythed out from him nonetheless.

Robin cowered his head into her. One ear nestling against her dress, the other blocked by his hand. Not wanting to see or hear any of this, but surely unable to ignore it.

Holding herself steady, Simone opened her mouth to respond, but the voices from the walls roared in unison:

"Veronique Salamone!"

As much as she had prepared herself, she saw a brief flash of beauty. A magnificent figure and soft, plump lips. She had been a bitch, but she was a one in sixty-seven million looker.

However, after the pleasure came the pain. Suddenly she saw Veronique with her eyes blackened by the boorish husband who she'd disappointed. A husband she'd sent Simone's picture to as Simone slept. Simone's profile in repose, peaceful and almost angelic; the blanket arranged so her naked right breast was part of the package. It had happened many times before that she'd enticed a lady home for them to share. In fact, these days, it was the only thing which brought them together. This time however, she'd left him frustrated and his rage had bubbled up. He hit once, twice, three times. Left her crumpled and weeping on their hallway floor. Their daughter saw all, but knew better than to try to comfort her mother. It would make Papa really mad. The problems in their marriage had been there a long time. Perhaps this was the last straw. Eventually he would kill her and leave her body in the bathtub with fifty different broken bones. Their daughter would discover it, while he made a run for the Spanish border.

How much of this was real? She saw it, but doubted it in the same instant. Fake news! Knew the house was trying to fuck with her.

"Helga Novak!" the voices screamed.

She relived them, but too briefly – the vibrations of sheer pleasure which Helga had given her. The pull of her heart at what she'd felt for the woman. *Still* felt for her.

But then there was sadness and unbelievable pain. Helga arriving home, smiling, determined to tell the woman she'd fallen madly in love with just what was in her heart. Only to find said woman had disappeared without even a note. There followed weeks of heartbreak. Days when this dedicated lady could not bring herself to go to work, letting her vocation slide. She'd never talked to Simone of her teenage depression. It was years ago, and she'd considered it behind her. But now she climbed into a bathtub of scalding water and swallowed a handful of sleeping pills. Then let herself sink until her face was below the surface and she had no strength to force her way to air.

Fantasy, surely. But Simone knew what was coming next.

"Lizzie Williamson!"

The gentleness of the shy young woman. How much affection she had harboured for Simone.

Simone's disappearance made her more reckless. She came to the realisation that life all alone wasn't worth living. There might be gossip and snide remarks, but she needed a companion to love. So Lizzie had forced herself to be brave. There had been one evening when friends had persuaded her to dress sexily and go to a bar, and that night she'd met the beautiful, sexy, charming Simone. Maybe it could happen again. And this time the woman she met would stay.

(How could Simone leave? Although she'd expected it, how could it actually happen?)

She went out a lot, drank too much, hunted for the love she thought she'd found with Simone. What happened to her was an accident, nobody's fault. One night she took hedonism too far. She wanted to fit in with a cool, young, peroxide blonde who was flirting with her. So she drank a lot and took a pill she shouldn't have. The blonde disappeared elsewhere and Lizzie went home alone. Unfortunately, in the morning, she didn't wake. It was the first weekend of the school summer holiday, so it was a full five days before they discovered her.

The visions disappeared and she was conscious of Robin squirming, then realised how tightly she was squeezing him. She missed both Lizzie and Helga an incredibly painful amount. Couldn't bear the thought of anything happening to either of them. Even Veronique – she never expected to see the woman again, but wanted her to stay safe.

All the house showed her didn't happen because of her, she was sure of it. In fact, she was confident it hadn't happened at all.

("But what if it had?" came a querulous voice within.)

"Murdering, cunting dyke bitch!" the voices around her yelled.

"How is it we can we help you, Miss?" Murkiss asked with undisguised impatience.

Simone raised her head slowly, kept her jaw level, not about to let Breakspear Hall twist around her mind anymore.

Her brother lay tight in her arms, her handbag rested against her thigh.

"Hello, gents." Her voice was defiantly strong. "I'm afraid all this has to come to an end."

CHAPTER FORTY-TWO

Murkiss chuckled to himself, a breathless sound which she could nevertheless hear above the shrieking from the walls. Then he bent his head slightly forward.

"And pray tell, what do you propose to do, Miss Simone? If you could illuminate me, I should be most grateful."

"What are you going to do?" echoed Robin.

The faces around the hallway cackled; dreadfully amused. "What are you going to do, you dyke bitch?"

Simone didn't react. Determinedly, she showed no fear. Just gazed into the frightened eyes of her brother. Kept his attention fixed on her.

"This has to end," she whispered to him.

"I know," he murmured. Before hurriedly adding: "I can do it. I have the time to figure a way."

She shook her head and tried to shush him. Robin kept talking though, panic rising:

"I can! I really can! If you help me, then we can work it out much faster. We can stop it. You know that. We're partners. We're a team. An exceptional team!"

The walls around cackled again. Mocking him, pricking at his confidence.

In her arms, he quaked. Her eyes narrowed and she leant in closer, not wanting to lose him to those screeching demons in the walls.

Softly she kissed him on the brow, then she whispered. She knew every word she uttered would be heard, but spoke as if it wasn't the case. "We are." she said. "We can take on anyone. We can take on the world."

Murkiss's lips didn't move, but the amusement was dripping from his entire being. "You are more than welcome to stay here if you wish, Miss Simone. The two of you can spend your days working it out together. You'll have time, I can promise you. Lots and lots of time." The last words echoed around the empty hallway, then were taken up as a chant by the faces on the walls.

"Si, talk to me," begged Robin. "What are you going to do?"

"Yes, what are you going to do, bitch?"

"It would delight us to know, Miss Simone." Murkiss's voice was only half a degree more pleasant than the others.

"I will rescue you from this," Simone whispered to Robin. "I should never have left my brother to suffer as you have. I should have saved you a long time ago. I will save you before it turns into an eternity."

"And how do you intend to achieve that, Miss Simone?"

The butler's face was craning so low she should have felt his breath on her brow. If he had any breath.

Robin peered at her. The same question unspoken on his lips, but she thought she could see – probably in spite of himself – a faint glimmer of hope somewhere deep in his eyes.

She feared Murkiss might react if she signalled her move, if she reached into her handbag too quickly. The round-faced bland malice would turn into a snarl the exact opposite of deference. As it was, his face was as aggressively curious as all his brethren in the walls. Dismissing her as a mere girl; amused that this silly chit would think she'd possess anything to match them. Confident she'd fail for them to witness. Give them something to convulse with laughter about.

A thousand times in LA, she'd held the sharp knives in the kitchen and imagined how she could end it. There were nights when she thought of ending herself too, but thankfully had resisted the urge. It was impossible for her to carry a big knife onto an aeroplane – particularly when she only had hand luggage. However, it was elementary to get the taxi driver to drop her at a kitchenware shop en route. It didn't cost much to buy herself a big, shiny, carving knife.

Her left hand whipped into her handbag and grabbed the hilt. (Her dread had been she'd slap her palm onto the blade itself). Then, before Murkiss could react, she pressed it to her brother's naked throat.

Robin gasped, his eyes bulging.

It was difficult to feel the surrounding room. There was surprise and an admiration she'd even threaten such a thing – but fear she'd actually do it? She didn't know. There was an apprehension, but it was combined with a morbid curiosity. She realised Breakspear Hall was daring her to slit its new master's throat. The house was wondering what its walls would look like when her brother's blood sprayed across them.

"You can't!" murmured Robin.

"There's no other way out of this torment. I can save you."

The only way to stop her hand trembling was to hold the blade as close as she could against his Adam's apple.

Naked and vulnerable on the floor, he winced. "I can save myself."

"Can you? After six months here, the life has been sucked from you. Imagine sixty years. Imagine an eternity."

"But if you did this, you…" He let the sentence trail off.

The butler remained hovering next to her, but she wasn't giving him the satisfaction of turning her head to regard him. Out of the corner of her eye though, did she imagine something akin to worry starting to creep onto his features?

He coughed politely. "The point I think Mr Robin is trying to make, Miss Simone is, if anything were to happen to him, you are his literal next of kin."

Robin's jaw tightened. Either because he didn't want the fact and the consequences of it spoken out loud, or she'd involuntarily pushed the blade another millimetre into his flesh.

Around her the cacophony of noise had lowered to a hush. The heads could barely move on the wall, but to her they were craning forward to see what happened next. Witnesses to, and participants of, a lurid soap opera.

Simone listened to her heartbeat in her skull and then held her breath to calm herself. Positive she was making the right decision, knowing it was too late to turn around and take flight.

Smiling as best she could, she leant in and kissed her brother on the lips. She hadn't done such a thing since they were children, so long ago.

"I'm sorry," she whispered. "But you will have to trust me. I was always the more resourceful one and you know it."

Then Simone dragged the knife left to right and slit open her brother's carotid artery.

The blade sank in deep. Piercing further than she thought it would. She'd imagined the muscle and gristle of a human throat would have made it a tough job, but it was like slicing through air. As if in her arms was already the ghost of Robin, rather than the man himself. The explosion of blood claimed otherwise though. It sprayed thick and viscous into her face, through her hair, onto her dress.

Unable to help herself, she screamed. Watching any colour drain from her brother's face, his limp body slipping from her arms and slumping to the floor. His head hit the bare wooden floorboards with a dull, wet thud.

The knife clattered beside her knees as she let go of the hilt – the plastic suddenly hot in her palm – but she didn't hear it. Instead, all around her was a vile, screeching laughter. The same word chanted in equal measures of hatred and triumph.

"Murderer! Murderer!"

CHAPTER FORTY-THREE

Simone was only thirty years old, but when she got to her feet, she creaked like an old biddy. Her head was swimming so much she thought she might come down again in a swoon.

Somehow she held herself together. She stayed up. Then she concentrated with every fragment of her being on the door ahead. It seemed to be swirling in the air, to be getting smaller and ever more distant.

The first couple of steps she took were tottering. She was hunched and weak at the hips, barely coordinated. Taking one deep, wheezy breath, she stopped, trying to right herself. Doing her utmost not to glance at Robin's corpse, there would be plenty of time to process that later. Instead, she focused her attention on the walls. At the thousands of male faces screaming at her. The gauntlet she had to traverse.

Blood was flowing thick from the walls. The squeezed out juices of a million corpses. It ran over their cheeks, across their faces, spewed from the mouths, sheathed their eyeballs, dripped from their brows. But their cruel, victorious screaming was unabated.

Her feet nearly slipped, and she realised the blood was flooding onto the floor. Between her and the door – which was flickering in and out in her fuzzy eyesight – was a river of red. Thick liquid; grime and gore floating within it. There were waves, she saw with a shudder. They were lapping back and fore across the hallway, detritus caught in the eddy. She could determine eyeballs, tongues, kidneys and hearts sloshing over the wooden floorboards and splashing towards her.

The scarlet covered eyes glared at her from the walls, their mouths spitting out red as they resounded with another chant:

"Heir! Heir! Heir!"

Simone took a step back, almost tumbling onto her arse. Only stopping when she hit the pudgy chest of Murkiss standing behind her.

She didn't thank him. Instead she jerked so far forward she nearly landed face first in the thick blood.

Of course he didn't feel the rebuff. Shimmering forward, he whispered in her ear: "Is there anything I can get for you, Miss Simone? I am eager to make you as comfortable as possible in your new home."

When she'd taken a step back, the vision of blood had faded a little. It wasn't as clear, not so real. Her joints had momentarily ceased aching.

If she retreated, gave herself to the house, then it would do its best to be beautiful for her. It would try to satisfy her desires. Decorate itself in the ways she wanted. Cost absolutely no object. It would offer her perfect lover after perfect lover. Maybe all she would eat from the kitchens would be her favourite meals and she'd never put on an extra pound. She could even lose the extra weight she had without exercising. There would be no faces in the walls, no screaming, no thick warm blood lapping around her ankles.

But what was the point of luxury if she had no one with whom to share it? What was the point of sex if love was absent?

How long would it really satisfy? After six months, Robin was completely broken. She doubted if her spirit would last six weeks.

Focusing, she lurched forward from Murkiss and took teetering steps, sloshing through the gore towards the doorway. Trying to picture where it should be, rather than where her eyes told her it currently appeared. What was in front of her wasn't real. Absolutely it was a kind of hell, but its power came from how she responded to it. The house wanted her to be afraid and cowed and to never venture towards the front door. A compliant, sated imbecile was all it desired. But if she didn't comply, it would never genuinely harm her. It couldn't harm her. There was no next of kin, there was only her and so she had to live. The sole way it could stop her was by frightening her. Just as it terrified and tormented Breakspear, then trapped Robin.

Half a dozen steps forward now. She could feel the blood warm on her calves. The smell of it coppery, with the added odour of excrement. Bowels and their voided contents caught in the flotsam. She kept moving, not raising her feet too high lest an amputated organ squelched beneath her heel and sent her sprawling.

"You know you can't truly leave us, Miss Simone." Murkiss was suddenly beside her, his tone pleasant and conversational. She didn't glance at his face.

Those faces on the walls more than made obvious what the house truly felt. The closer to the door she managed, the more hate-filled they became. She tried not to glance at them, not wanting to be caught in the fury of their expressions. Fearful if she cast her eyes across them, she'd recognise Robin's face. And it would be as full of contempt and judgement as the others.

"Previous masters have tried to go their own paths, Miss Simone. The fact is though, this is your home, and like all homes – all *true* homes – you can never really leave it. If you go through the door, we will never leave you. We will accompany you everywhere. A constant reminder that your rightful place in the universe is here. In Breakspear Hall. With us."

Every step was a struggle. Her limbs were aching. Even her face was pained. The determination she wore grinding at her teeth. Already she could feel the allure of youth leaving her, her smooth skin wrinkling way beyond her years. Curiosity made her want to touch it, to see how bad the damage was, but simple vanity would not stop her progress.

"You can have a good life here," Murkiss assured her. "I think I mentioned before that your predilections will make your time here easier to accommodate. The Mr Breakspears and your brother were all fine red-blooded men. They knew what they liked when it came to the ladies, and those of us in the house made sure they were extremely satisfied. Miss Helga can be here for you, Miss Lizzie too. Together, even. Both of them wrapped around you for as a long as you desire."

His tone had become unctuous again, but the sheer

sleaziness of his words disgusted her as much as the blood and offal drifting by her ankles.

One of the faces to her left screamed directly at her. Louder than the others, more familiar. She couldn't help turning her head.

It was her father. Daddy. His absent-minded, friendly expression replaced by one of utter hostility to his only daughter. He and Robin had always rubbed the wrong way across each other, but she'd known she was adored. Now the idea raced through her mind unbidden: "*Daddy hates me!*"

Quickly she dismissed it. So as not to get distracted, not to crumple inside. She snapped her head away and fixed in her mind where the front door should be. It wasn't real. None of this was real.

The noise became more intense. Ten thousand voices yelling and chanting at her. The word "Murderer" she heard, along with "Dyke", "Bitch" and "Successor". All those voices, with burning hatred mixed together and aimed solely at her.

Despite having waded into the gore with her, Murkiss's suit remained unblemished. His tone, although reaching for calm, contained an undeniable irritation. "You cannot leave us, Miss Simone. It's silly for you to imagine you can."

Incredibly, she'd done it. She had made it through the river of blood and shit. The front door was before her. Not moving now, and not an illusion.

Trembling, her hand reached for the handle. At first it slipped from her grasp. It was too smeared with bodily fluids, impossibly slippery to the touch. That was the moment when all hope could have disappeared from her, her legs folding beneath her body. Even at the doorway, she couldn't escape. Desperately she steadied herself, trying to believe that the house couldn't really stop her. As she did, she glanced upwards. There, above the door – mounted as the biggest tiger killed on a hunt – was Robin.

His eyes were wide and bulging, but the blood wasn't running across his face from the walls. It was spurting like a fountain from his exposed throat. Spraying onto her again, covering her hair and clothes with her brother's still warm life-blood.

Unable to help herself, she shrieked and nearly collapsed backwards. This time Murkiss wasn't behind her, but she just about kept her footing.

Forcing herself forward, arms out, she took a two-handed grip on the handle and closed her eyes.

None of it was real. All she had to do was turn the handle and she was as free as she would ever be.

Over her shoulder, Murkiss's voice boomed along with every other man within the walls. "You are the successor! Breakspear Hall wants you!"

For a first time in a long while she smiled and truly meant it. "I might be the successor," she told him, yanking open the door. "But the thing is, I don't want Breakspear Hall. It's not really my taste."

Then, with the house's rage a tornado behind her, she stepped outside and slammed the door as hard as she could. It gave a sickening thud.

On increasingly weary limbs, Simone hobbled down the driveway. An old lady wearing a black dress far too young for her, one whose material fortunately hid most stains. The evening was drawing in and drizzle was in the air. She hoped that when she finally reached the road, it wouldn't take too long to find a taxi.

CHAPTER FORTY-FOUR

A mere ten days later, an impossibly old looking lady sat at a table in a Munich pavement café. Her skin was leathery and cracked, her hair wisps to her head, while her lips had faded to next to nothing. Any estimation of her age would have put her at a hundred at least. Possibly this would be a conservative guess. There was a light in her eyes though. It would be difficult to describe it as a zest for life, but it was undoubtedly determination.

She sat in a straight-backed wheelchair. Trying to keep as upright as possible, a glass of peach schnapps so far untouched in front of her.

A man had followed her in. Letting the lady's old and arthritic fingers push the wheels of the chair, while never hiding the fact he was with her. Obviously not concerned about the unpleasant looks he received as a consequence. He was a bald man with a bland face, and he wore a fine suit and stood deferentially behind her. If you hadn't watched her wheel herself painfully through the door, you might have believed he was her carer. Until you saw his expression and realised how little he cared.

Whatever. She ignored him.

Instead, the old lady watched the passers-by. Hunting for someone she knew. A person who never came to this particular café, but lived five minutes' walk from it, with her favourite delicatessen five minutes on the other side. All being well, she'd stroll by at some point.

The old lady didn't have to wait long to give a gasp of recognition. Genuine pleasure crinkling her aged face.

What she saw was a particularly attractive young couple. One of them an athletic lady with short auburn hair, holding hands with a gorgeous dark-skinned woman, her own hair swinging in a ponytail.

The old lady had no idea who this new beauty was and didn't care. At first glance she appeared pleasant, and the woman holding her hand was obviously smitten. It was wonderful to see them lost in their own private bubble. Grinning at each other and no one else. They completely missed the old lady's presence, not that the young woman with auburn hair would have recognised her anyway.

Seven days earlier in London, the same scenario had been almost repeated. Then the young lady hadn't been with a new lover, but she had been with friends and appeared happy.

At the airport, the old lady – who at that point had seemed vigorous enough not to need a wheelchair – had even gone online and checked for news of a certain French actress. There was nothing of note, she was pleased to see. Only an announcement that the new series of her TV show would be released soon.

She had also, in the five minutes when her now constant companion, had seemed to melt away, emailed Mr Burbank – her and her brother's solicitor on the South Coast. As quickly as she could, she gave him a set of instructions. There was an old house in Forest Hill in London she wanted demolished. He was to use the money from their charity to hire a bulldozer and a work crew and get it done forthwith. In her conversation with Montagu Breakspear, he had told her that the house couldn't be damaged. He had speculated that it couldn't even be bulldozed. Well, she'd see what the reality of ten tonnes of charging metal made of that.

Now, in the café, the man behind her – who was seemingly dressed as a butler or a valet – leant in and whispered a remark to her. The lasciviousness on his face made him resemble a demon offering temptation.

But it evidently didn't matter what he was saying. The old woman wasn't listening. Idly she wondered what would happen to him if her destructive plan was put into her action. Would he vanish into thin air? Or shriek curses as he tried to pull her back to his hell with him?

Or maybe he'd smile at her smugly because Breakspear's assertion had been correct all along.

She was curious to see which it would be. Knowing that either way, she was never going to get any younger.

With shaky fingers, she reached across and took her glass of schnapps. Almost upsetting it, before gripping the stem tight.

She raised it with painful slowness to her lips.

Toasting to the future, toasting love, toasting Breakspear Hall, which she would never ever see again. She toasted to the end.

A Note from the author

If you enjoyed Terror of Breakspear Hall, then do check out the other entries in The Ghostly Shadows series. The other terrifying instalments: Death at the Seaside, Certain Danger, Call of the Mandrake, The Hellbound Detective and The Caller are all now available in paperback. Each is ostensibly a standalone, but if you read them all you'll start to recognise the connections...

In addition, if you have read and enjoyed this novel, would you please take the time to leave a short review of it on Amazon?

Reviews are the lifeblood of an indie author. They make the difference between scrabbling along and actually making a living out of our writing. So, if you're able to find the time to leave your thoughts on Terror of Breakspear Hall – or any of my other Ghostly Shadows tales – then I would be tremendously grateful.

Kind regards,

FRJ.

OTHER BOOKS IN THE GHOSTLY SHADOWS SERIES

All available in paperback.

DEATH AT THE SEASIDE

Nothing was going to ruin Castle's holiday, except the mocking laughter of the dead…

Larry Castle was anticipating a lovely few days at the seaside. Basking in the sunshine, canoodling with his mistress and playing the big man visiting town. However, a chance encounter leaves his confidence reeling.

There's a possibility that someone knows his darkest secret. The thing that made him, but which could equally break him. No matter what, Castle is going to have to deal with this problem. Otherwise it could cost him everything.

This weekend Castle is going to confront the ghosts of his past, but some ghosts are more real than others…

The first in the Ghostly Shadows Anthology series.

CERTAIN DANGER

What are those voices from the past? And why are they screaming at her?

It all started when she witnessed a car crash. A brutal smash which left a gorgeous young couple dead. But for Alice, it reawakened strange memories of childhood: a sinister old house, a dead boy in the woods and an other-worldly power lurking forever in the darkness.

Desperate to make sense of the bizarre pictures in her mind, Alice's enquires lead her to a hidden away clinic in the Surrey Hills. Within those walls though, are the terrifying secrets she's been running from her whole life.

Now, for Alice, the truth could not only break apart her sanity, it could destroy the whole world…

The second in the Ghostly Shadows Anthology series.

CALL OF THE MANDRAKE

What terrible secrets are the town's women hiding?

Beddnic, on the South Wales coast, has shut itself off from the outside world. Days after a number of its men were reported missing, the road in was closed and all communications ceased. No strangers are welcome there anymore.

Now, two agents – Ludo and Mick – are venturing across the water, anxious to know what's going on and desperate to help. And no amount of threats or horrors will make them turn back. The awful curse which has befallen this town is about to be revealed, and the dead shall walk…

But in this cruel place by the sea, will these two men really be able to help?

The third in the Ghostly Shadows Anthology series.

THE HELLBOUND DETECTIVE

He's on the path to hell, but does he have a shot at salvation?

Algernon Swafford has returned to the city of his birth. Only now London is bombed out and on its knees. Deep down Swafford feels the same. This once great private detective is a wreck. He's trapped in the employ of a demon of a man. One skilled in other-worldly magic, who revels in every sin and depravity.

However, on the brutal streets of an English winter, Swafford spies a chance to save himself. His master has enemies and these enemies have their own powers. He can use them to save himself. But can he do it without them using him?

Suddenly caught in the middle of an other-worldly conflict on London's streets, Swafford knows if he can hold his nerve and keep himself alive, he might just have a chance at saving his soul. First though, he'll have to face creatures from the darkest part of man's imagination…

Can Swafford rescue himself? Or will he be damned for eternity?

Noir, fantasy and horror collide in the fourth of the Ghostly Shadows series!

THE CALLER

Meeting him will make this the deadliest night of your life!

A series of bizarre, violent murders shocks London. The victims all seemingly unconnected, apart from the brutality of their deaths. Each demise is more gruesome than the last. A card, perfectly red on each side, is discovered with every corpse.

Jenna Driscoll, a young crime blogger, begins to investigate. But what she finds seems beyond comprehension. A supernatural demon summoned from the pages of an old horror novel, who will kill eight people across eight nights in increasingly horrific ways.

Every police officer and crime investigator in the city is drawn into the case, but there seems no way of finding him. Let alone stopping his carnage. However, Jenna is about to discover a far more terrible truth. That if you investigate deep enough, and gain his attention, you can add yourself to his bloody list…

As he is The Caller, and when he visits, it means death!

The sixth in the Ghostly Shadows Anthology series.

ALSO BY F.R. JAMESON THE SCREEN SIREN NOIR SERIES

All available in paperback.

DIANA CHRISTMAS

He's been threatened, beaten and broken – but still he doesn't regret meeting the actress who disappeared...

Michael, a young film journalist, is sent to interview the reclusive movie star Diana Christmas. Twenty years prior, the red-headed starlet suddenly abandoned her career, leaving her fans puzzled and shocked.

Their attraction is instant. Between the sheets, Diana tells him of the blackmail and betrayal which ruined her. And how – even now – she's being tormented.

Emboldened, Michael sets out on a mission to track down a compromising roll of film – unaware that around the next corner lurks deadly peril.

Can Michael save Diana from her past? Or will the secrets which crushed her life destroy them both?

Diana Christmas: Blackmail, Death and a British Film Star – a new thriller of desire and betrayal from F.R. Jameson.

The first in the Screen Siren Noir series.

EDEN ST. MICHEL

Avenging her secret could put a noose around both their necks…

Joe might be a stuntman, but still he'd never expect to end up in bed with a genuine movie star. However, that's what happens the night he meets the ultra-glamorous, Eden St. Michel. Swiftly they're the talk of the town. Their passion fast, intense and dangerous.

But Eden has scars from her past, both mental and physical. Joe needs to be her hero, although retribution won't be easy. One misstep could mean the end of their careers and – maybe – their lives.

After a sudden moment of violence, Joe finds himself in deadly trouble. He may have the love of a good woman, yet it's leading him to the gallows.

But what if the only way to save Eden is to make that ultimate sacrifice?

Eden St. Michel: Scandal, Death and a British Film Star – a new tale of film stars, gangsters and death from F.R. Jameson.

The second book in the 'Screen Siren Noir' series.

ALICE RACKHAM

Theirs is an affair destined to end in murder!

Thomas had never met a woman like Alice Rackham. A film-star: sophisticated and uninhibited. Not only is their passion intense, but she could help this impoverished young actor with his own career. Surely it doesn't really matter that she has danger written all over her…

As he isn't the only one smitten with Alice: her ex-lover skulks ceaselessly outside her home and keeps a former policeman on retainer. A giant of a man who would relish making both their lives torture.

With Thomas rattled, Alice suggests a relaxing trip to an English country house. But trouble isn't just going to follow them out there, it's about to turn deadly.

Can Thomas save Alice from her past? Or will it destroy them both?

Alice Rackham: Obsession, Death and a British Film Star - a new thriller of passion, jealousy and suspense from F.R. *Jameson.*

The third novel in the Screen Siren Noir series.

ABOUT THE AUTHOR

F.R. Jameson was born in Wales, but now lives with his wife and daughter in London. He writes thrillers; sometimes of the supernatural variety, and sometimes historical, set around the British film industry.

His debut novel, The Wannabes, which contains both horror and British actresses is available for free now from his blog, which you can find at - https://frjameson.com/

You can also find him on Facebook, and follow him on Twitter, Instagram and Pinterest: @frjameson.

Printed in Great Britain
by Amazon

64166346R00180